EVERYONE'S THINKING IT

EVERYONE'S THINKING IT

Aleema Omotoni

Balzer + Bray

An Imprint of HarperCollins*Publishers*

Balzer + Bray is an imprint of HarperCollins Publishers.

Everyone's Thinking It
Copyright © 2023 by Aleema Omotoni
All rights reserved. Printed in the United States of America.
No part of this book may be used or reproduced in any manner whatsoever
without written permission except in the case of brief quotations embod-
ied in critical articles and reviews. For information address HarperCollins
Children's Books, a division of HarperCollins Publishers, 195 Broadway,
New York, NY 10007.
www.epicreads.com

Library of Congress Control Number: 2023932460
ISBN 978-0-06-322567-1

Typography by Corina Lupp
23 24 25 26 27 LBC 5 4 3 2 1

First Edition

Dedicated with love to my mum, whose goodness and patience knows no bounds. You are warmth personified. May God grant you the highest blessings in this life and the next.

For Black girls of all ages. I see your softness, I see your light. You are love and deserve an entire world of it.

A Note from the Author

The weight of experiences we carry can often be reflected in the themes of the stories we read. This book explores themes around race, class, gender, sexuality, and mental health; all of which, I've tried my best to handle with great care. As such, discussions and depictions of anti-Black racism, blackface, blackfishing, colorism, misogynoir, biphobia, queerphobia, sexism, and panic attacks are present in this novel. You know best what weights you carry, so I hope that you take care of yourself if you decide to journey into this story.

ONE

Iyanu

There are just these little things that a camera lens can reveal about a person. Things that they don't want anyone else to see. And when you're the one with the camera, you tend to fade into the background. You get to be part of the world without having to be a part of the world.

Exactly how I like it.

I've always preferred working with film; something about the way it captures light feels so alive. The first time I ever printed photos, I was ten. Now, seven years later, the carefully controlled process is practically embedded into each line on my palms, and I go through the motions with ease. It's just as practiced as taking the photos themselves, the comforting familiarity of creating something new. Revealing hidden truths in a way that only the process of exposure can achieve.

But unlike ten-year-old Iyanu in the makeshift darkroom that Mum, Dad, and I put together in our tiny downstairs bathroom, I'm now in the Wodebury Hall photography lab, surrounded by stainless steel surfaces laden with expensive tools and devices.

Adjusting my glasses, I peg a photo up onto the drying line behind me and consider the perspective in the red glow of the gently buzzing safety light. It's a picture I'd taken yesterday of the matchmaking event we'd held in the fields behind Wodebury House, the main school building.

Despite being a frigid Friday evening in late January, we'd had a great turnout. In the photo, a good chunk of the Year Twelve boarders and some of my fellow day students stand bundled up among the trees in stylish knit jumpers and tweed coats, like outfits straight out of a designer winter collection.

And most of them probably are.

Each round of the matchmaking event had one contestant and twelve potential matches. The event's host asked both groups specifically themed questions on everything from favorite color to relationship dealbreakers. After each question, the contestant eliminated potential matches based on the compatibility of their answers until there was only one person left.

I glance over the photo again, scanning the faces of every person on the stage. The lens reveals their stories, the slight nervousness concealed behind the participants' beaming expressions, the anticipation glimmering in the eyes of the students who came to watch.

A committee of Year Twelve students always puts together the Valentine's Day Ball for Sixth Formers—the Year Twelves and Year Thirteens—that will be happening in two weeks, and I'd been unexpectedly nominated to the group by our head of year to oversee all photography matters. And when this matchmaking event had been proposed as a fun way for us Year Twelve students to find dates for said ball, I'd been the only person on the committee who didn't see the point of it.

However, as each couple was matched throughout the evening, the point quickly became clear: conflict and drama. Which can be entertaining—everyone loves a good soapy spectacle—but it's exactly the kind of situation I'd normally avoid for the sake of my own mental health.

Once I set the final matchmaking print to rinse for a few minutes, I'm eager to pour over the images I'd rather be working on instead. So I hurry over to the cubby shelf where I'd kept my things.

I grab my film negative binder and a magnifying glass, then quickly flip to the pages where I'd stored my negatives from the Black Girls Winter Fair.

Warmth fills my chest.

The fair had taken place in London last weekend, and I'd been staring at the negatives every chance I could this entire week, anticipating the moment when I could finally print my favorites. Unfortunately, the matchmaking photos needed to take priority.

The photo rinse timer starts beeping when I get to the final one, the image distorted by the glaze of unshed tears around my eyes. I ignore the sound, staring at the image for a little longer with an achingly wide smile.

It was the best moment of the entire weekend. I was heading out of the fair when I'd spotted my favorite writer, Kia Rose, an amazing photojournalist and professor of Black women's history.

After building up the courage to speak to her, she'd let me take a photo of her standing in front of the Wall of Messages; the place where my own tear-stained note was pinned up alongside those of the other fair attendees with messages of love about their time spent that weekend.

I'd already planned to use these photos for my *WeCreate* article—the final stage in the application process for the online magazine's photojournalist position. But seeing Kia Rose that day felt like fate.

I'd discovered the magazine in Year Seven, marveling at the space created by queer women of color writing about their passions and experiences. The first issue I'd ever read was guest edited by Kia Rose, and I can never forget that feeling of being so completely seen, even though my eleven-year-old self hadn't fully processed the importance of having a safe haven away from Wodebury's halls. Now that I do, I just need to write about it, that same feeling captured here in every image I'd taken at the fair: Black women celebrating in community.

Nervous anticipation rushes down my spine, followed by a twinge of desperation.

The job is perfect anyway, but I also just need it. Wodebury giving me a bursary to cover the fees to study here is one thing, but the upkeep of being here is another—I wouldn't even be able to afford the ticket to the

Valentine's Day Ball if I didn't have a discount as a committee member. I need as much extra income as I can get.

My thoughts are interrupted by several successive dings of text notifications.

I quickly return the negative strip to the binder and head back to the processing station, grateful for my phone's darkroom filter as I open up the messages.

Saturday 8:07 P.M.

Nav

> no, i won't stop pouting! you'd feel the exact same way if you had a dream match and that happened to you 😣

> i just wish Jordan didn't leave . . . Mr. Leighton said everyone on the committee had to take part yesterday, i needed the plausible deniability

Navin had only joined the committee to keep me from being alone with the "popular crew," but he'd spent most of his time subtly eyeing Jordan.

Another message comes in, and I laugh at the selfie of Navin's pouting face. The soft pink gloss on his lips shines perfectly against his light bronze skin, and from the background, it seems like he's returned to his dorm room in Roweton House.

Navin—and access to this darkroom—are my saving graces here at Wodebury Hall. He'd spent most of his early life shuttling between England, Bangladesh, and another boarding school in Spain before arriving at Wodebury Hall in Year Nine. His mum, the owner of a multimillion-dollar international architecture firm that builds large-scale city projects, was born and raised in Bangladesh, while his dad is Bengali and white British aristocracy. So Navin and his father stand to inherit an estate from Navin's grandfather, who he often describes as "an old white man who means well but is still an old white man."

> sorry babe

> but you know what? here's a wild idea, what if you just *ask* Jordan to the ball?

Navin's response comes in immediately, and I chuckle.

> i hate you

> i just want to tell him how pretty he is . . . but like, i also never want to tell him how pretty he is 😫

The words hit a little too close to home, and I hurriedly ignore the face they conjure up, the memories threatening at the edge of my mind.

> you love me, i'm your favorite person 😄

> unfortunately . . .

I laugh gleefully at the voice note that follows of a deep resigned sigh.

> i love you

> i love you too 😌

Smirking, I put the phone down, only to have the mirth disappear at the sight of the completed image staring back at me in the wash tank.

I'd purposefully left this photo for last because I hadn't wanted to take it in the first place.

There are only three subjects. My cousin Kitan Ladipo and her two best friends, Sarah Pelham and Heather Seymour-Cavendish. The trio stand in their default pose with Heather in the center, her green eyes glinting in the reflection of the large bonfire lit for the matchmaking event.

I can still hear Heather's annoyingly saccharine tone asking me to take the photo of them. She'd walked up to me, dripping with the type of confidence that can only come from believing that no one would ever deny you anything.

And as an earl's daughter, most people never dare.

For example, on the committee, she'd been the one to come up with the matchmaking event idea. And even though everyone else had readily agreed, she'd posed it as a statement, not a question.

My sigh comes out like a growl. Looking at this photo, I can clearly see that no one has ever told her that blackfishing is wrong either.

Heather came back at the start of this school year from a summer away on safari in Kenya, apparently having decided that blackfishing was where it was at. She'd permed her dark brown hair into tightly spiraled curls to "go with" her fresh tan, employing the makeup skills that had earned her over two hundred thousand followers and subscribers across her social media platforms to make her skin look even browner. Her tan has definitely long since faded, but with the help of a foundation shade that would be more at home on my dressing table, she always ensures that her white skin is just bronzed enough for her to appear "exotic Black."

Her racist words, not mine.

That first day, I'd preemptively decided I was too exhausted to deal with all that mess. Heather has hated me since the day we met, and it'd be a waste of my precious time and labor trying to educate her.

But as I examine the image now, noting the shade of her heavily bronzed skin next to Sarah's pale white—Heather's real skin color—it's become evident that Heather is getting way too close to the line of blatant blackface.

Now I definitely have to do something, or at least say something to Kitan.

I should have sensed all this coming after Year Eleven when Heather had gotten her results from a DNA test. Because even though it showed that she was completely Western European with a "trace amount of undetermined ancestry," like most white people on Earth, she'd gone on and on about how she had no idea she was "mixed."

Rolling my eyes, I hang up the photo to dry and my gaze lingers on Kitan.

Much like every day since Heather came to Wodebury in Year Nine, and especially since I joined the ball committee, I just can't help but wish that Kitan didn't hang out with them—Heather, Sarah, and the rest of "the popular kids." But I suppose with Kitan, old habits always die hard. And there's no way she'd hang out with me either way.

Not anymore.

I glance at the photo hanging next to the trio, the one I'd captured of Kitan at the exact moment she was matched with Oliver Wei last night. The firelight dances in her eyes, orange hues bouncing off her skin like sparkles of gold.

It was a happy surprise when they were paired. During our first few years at Wodebury, when Kitan and I were still close, I noticed that everyone started dating each other while the two of us remained perpetually single. As the only two highly melanated Black girls in our year at a primarily white boarding school in the countryside of southeast England, it seemed that no one was going to be looking our way.

Kitan had to have noticed too, but we've never talked about it.

There's a lot of stuff we don't talk about.

But unlike me, who'd resigned myself to being solitary in all aspects of my life, Kitan wasn't one to give up on love.

So she'd spent the whole evening with a smile, making sure the long dark brown waves of her wig and the loose curls of the parted curtain fringe were sitting just so.

I'm happy that it ultimately worked out for her, even with the sadness that still lingers after everything that's happened between us—just as happy as she'd looked walking off the stage with Oliver.

I guess my old habits die hard too.

And not just with Kitan.

My traitorous eyes scan the drying line, searching for the face I've been trying to ignore since I'd developed the photo.

Quincy.

The tiny ache that blooms in my chest feels a little too much like mourning, but my thoughts are mercifully interrupted again by the sharp dinging of texts, this time from Mum asking when I'm coming home.

After shooting back a reply, I quickly clear up the chemicals and wash my hands. I take one last look at the pages of the Black Girls Winter Fair negatives then place the binder underneath my camera bag in the cubby shelf, ready to go first thing on Monday morning since the darkroom is closed tomorrow.

As I head toward the exit, I glance around the red-lit room at the photos hanging from the line, then grab my satchel and shut off the safe light.

The smell of chemicals is strong in the air as I inhale a deep breath, steeling myself to leave this peaceful space, before heading out the revolving doors.

The photography lab is located in the art department in Wodebury House, the massive four-wing neoclassical building that houses most of the school's main classrooms. As I hurry through the long-shadowed hallways, the giant windows offer glimpses of the two nearest dorm buildings:

Lady Chalford House and Brookfield House. The former a late-Victorian redbrick mansion with carved white stone facings, and the latter a large stone building with a classic symmetrical Regency facade.

And that's what gives Wodebury its charm—an eclectic collection of buildings from all the different eras the school has seen in its three hundred years, chronicling the spread and growth of the ancient institution.

So maybe *charm* isn't the right word.

My footsteps echo on the marble floors before disappearing into the night air that bites coolly at the skin of my cheeks as I exit the building. Hugging my oversized coat tighter around myself, I head down the large front steps and into the courtyard. Wodebury House, with its Corinthian columns of cream stone and ornate sculpted wreaths, seems to glow in the moonlit sky.

The stars always look beautiful from here, and I trace their familiar patterns as I cross over the cobblestoned ground toward the parking lot. Pulling my scarf over my chilled nose, the barrier sends my panting breaths upward, fogging over my glasses as I start to turn the corner.

"Oof!"

Before I can fall backward, whoever I'd slammed into grabs my shoulders to steady me.

"Sorry!"

The familiar voice sends a shiver scattering down my arms, and I pull off my fogged-over glasses before looking up at Quincy's slightly blurry form.

His surprised expression melts into a tiny smile. "Iyanu. You okay?"

Willing my heart to slow down, I rub my arm where we made impact.

"Y-Yeah, that was partly my fault," I stumble out, gesturing upward. "Got a little distracted."

Quincy glances up at the sky with a chuckle. Putting on a deeper voice, he declares, *"'Ill met by moonlight.'"*

It takes only a second for me to place the Shakespeare quote, another to realize the "ill met" he's talking about is our collision, and one more to remember that we'd rewatched *A Midsummer Night's Dream* at our final movie marathon. And then the ache flares again.

I'm bombarded by a series of memories I always try to keep buried: The chubby-cheeked seven-year-old who'd smiled happily at me on the playground our mums had brought us to. A smile that led to four years of inseparable friendship before we all came to Wodebury and everything changed. The shy little kid I'd spent every weekend with for seven years—even as we found ourselves interacting less and less at school during the last three—baking cookies and having movie marathons in the makeshift blanket fort on his bedroom floor; the film projected on the blank wall above his desk.

And then the newest memory haunting me: Quincy being paired with Heather at the matchmaking event after all the other people had been eliminated from his round. I'd managed to capture the image as it happened.

He'd tried to keep a straight face, but I'd like to believe my lens was right when it revealed the resignation in his eyes. The reluctant acceptance. Typical Quincy, who would never want to make a scene.

My musings plunge us into an awkward silence, and I fiddle with the arms of my glasses to distract myself from the acute pang of these reminders.

Quincy and I are voracious readers, and back in the old days, whenever Quincy would randomly come out with literary quotes, I'd respond with where it was from. But we don't do this anymore. Since we both joined the committee, Quincy and I have shared a few words here and there—and one lingering glance when he suggested Old Hollywood for the ball's theme—but before that . . . not since Year Nine.

Quincy clears his throat, gesturing his chin over my shoulder. "Did you get through the matchmaking photos?"

I nod shakily. "You coming from Brookfield? Still about an hour or two left till weekend curfew, right?"

"Yeah, I was just heading to the library. Jordan wanted some chocolate, and you know how he only ever eats Kit Kats, but the Brookfield common room has run out."

In December, right at the end of Michaelmas term, Jordan fractured his ankle in a rugby match and has to stay in a cast for another week. So Quincy's going all the way to the library vending machines to get one of his brothers a Kit Kat.

My heart, which had finally started settling down, kicks up a notch again.

"Is everything okay with Jordan? I know he left the matchmaking event early."

I was once nearly as close to Quincy's younger twin brothers, Jordan and Marcus, as I was to him. So the concern is genuine, even if a tiny part of me is still scoping out the situation for Nav.

"Yeah, Jordie's all right."

Nodding, I wipe down my glasses and put them back on.

Quincy's face comes into crystal focus. His large dark brown eyes framed with thick brows and even darker long lashes, intense against the warm brown of his skin. The line of his button nose leading down to big pouty lips with a tiny fading scar in the corner. The sharp, lightly bearded jawline.

It's all just too Quincy, and I have to drop my gaze to my penny loafers. But that doesn't stop me from also noticing how unfairly good he looks in the navy suit and red-striped rugby tie he's wearing.

Focus.

". . . but I dunno," he continues, oblivious to my distracted musings. "I'm just a little worried about the twins."

My laughter comes without my permission, and I lift my eyes once again.

Quincy is always worried about Jordan and Marcus. The Villar twins have always had a way of getting into trouble.

I say as much, and Quincy lets out a breathy chuckle. "Yeah, I guess."

Another silence, this time a little suffocating.

"Okay, I'm just gonna . . ." I trail off, pointing ahead.

"Yeah! Yeah, okay, see you on Monday."

Then we do this weird dance thing where we both try to go around the other in the same direction. After two false starts, I grab his shoulders gently—trying not to focus on the heat radiating through his soft wool coat—and maneuver us around.

Quincy chuckles again, running a hand over his dark curls, which are loose and free. "See you later."

I wait for a few moments until he disappears into the building before heading on my way.

TWO

Kitan

Oliver

> should i come pick you up from Brookfield? or do you want to meet at the practice rooms?

Even in text, I can hear the cadence of Oliver's voice. The deep tenor that always sends warmth rushing through me.

It's *so* easy to grin wide and a little goofy when it comes to Oliver. To just let my guard down. But before the corners of my mouth can even begin to inch upward, I remember where I am, surrounded by way too many people to do that kind of thing.

In my absentmindedness as we'd been texting back and forth, the careful positioning of my face is all wrong now, my hair is probably a mess, my blouse—

Taking a breath, I school my face back to my usual neutral expression, automatically filing my feelings away.

Not here. Never here.

It takes a second longer than usual, but I successfully compartmentalize my thoughts, smooth down my hair, and adjust my blouse before responding to Oliver's message with an affirmative.

The common room at Brookfield House is a grand space, with intricately carved rosettes in the high light wood ceiling, an entire wall of floor-to-ceiling bookcases, and heavy jacquard curtains. It sports a blend of the old and new: leather chesterfield sofas, a wood-carved pool table, and a grand piano in one corner, alongside a flat-screen television with game consoles, vending machines, and foosball tables. Naturally, this always draws a Saturday evening horde, which, combined with the blazing fireplace, means the room is a bit too warm, and I discreetly wipe at my brow.

Even with the crowd, Sarah, Heather, and I have easily managed to snag the long sofa near the pool table to ourselves.

Everyone knows that's where we sit.

I try to file away the twinge of guilt I feel at what it took to get here, because the alternative feels much worse. Being relegated to the fringes of Wodebury's social life. Laughed at. Before Year Nine, people would have looked at me sideways the moment I walked into this room. With Sarah and Heather, none of that happens.

Yes. This is leagues better.

"Who're you texting?"

Heather's voice comes from my right. Her tone is almost purposefully laced with slight boredom. Like she doesn't want to seem too interested.

I hope that the way my shoulders tense as I tilt the phone away doesn't make it too obvious that I'm trying to keep her from seeing the screen.

"Just Oliver," I respond softly.

Oliver could never be *just* anything, but it's the only thing I can think of to say.

The teasing smile of Heather's newly plumped lips, unnatural against the equally unnatural bronze of her skin, doesn't fully reach her eyes. "Oh, so now that you both have dates to the ball, you no longer have time for me?"

From Heather's other side, Sarah looks up from her phone with an amused eye roll. I hold in my giggle as we exchange a quick look.

The matchmaking event had been Heather's idea. As committee

president, it didn't take much for her to convince our head of year, Mr. Leighton, to let it go ahead. But he'd stipulated that all committee members had to take part, "in the interest of community spirit and engagement." Iyanu was exempt though, so she could take the photos. A part of me had wished I could be too. Instead, I spent the night terrified and bracing for the usual rejection, only this time on a much more public stage. But after almost an entire evening of the expected disappointment . . . Oliver.

"You say that like you're not going with Quincy," Sarah responds, tucking a strand of brunette hair behind her ear. But as she turns to face Heather, leaning back against the sofa arm, her bob shakes and the strand falls free again, brushing her pale white freckled cheek. "I was just double-checking my game plan for Wednesday."

It's a Saturday evening, and Sarah is working on her color coded down-to-the-minute calendar that she created for this term. I smile at the endearing familiarity. It's all an effort to optimize her chances at getting nominated to run for head girl next year. This most recent hurdle is the head girl workshop on Career Day. All prospective applicants will be attending to impress Mr. Leighton, who, as our head of year, has the biggest sway in the teachers' nomination process.

"Yeah," Heather starts, inspecting her nails. "I was thinking of going to the workshop on Wednesday too."

There's a moment of silence as Sarah blinks confusedly. "Why?"

My shoulders tense a little more.

Heather, seemingly oblivious to Sarah's silent freak-out, continues picking at her nail polish. "For all the head girl stuff, right? I told you I was gonna try for it last week, didn't I?"

She did. But neither Sarah nor I thought she was actually being serious.

Ever since Year Seven, Sarah has always had top marks in every one of her classes, all while creating the perfect résumé with a host of extracurriculars and the titles prefect, subject leader, and student council member under her belt. All this would make her an excellent choice to be nominated by the teachers and, if everything goes according to plan with her campaign next year, to win.

I'd briefly considered running for head girl a few years ago. But when I realized how important it was to Sarah, I decided against it. She has Wodebrians all the way up her family tree from both her parents, and all the women on her mother's side have *always* made head girl. Ever since her parents split when she was ten and she started living with her dad and stepmother, she's been fiercely determined to make sure the tradition remained unbroken.

Besides, even if I was nominated by the teachers, no one would vote for me. Not with the types of numbers Sarah could get. And definitely nowhere near the type of landslide Heather Seymour-Cavendish could achieve.

"Right," Sarah says, staring at her phone like she's trying to convince herself that this new reality doesn't exist. "But you haven't been going to any of the meetings and stuff. Have you even signed up for the workshop?"

Heather nods, finally looking up from her nails with a grin. "Yup! Got in just before the deadline yesterday. I'm *this* close to landing a cool new brand deal, but I'll be able to balance it all." Sarah's responding smile looks a little constipated, but she doesn't get a chance to respond over the sudden jeers that erupt.

All the rugby players, sans Quincy, who is off searching for Jordan's Kit Kat, are draped over the sofas and armchairs in front of the fireplace. They'd been playing pool, but now Jordan, Marcus, and Luc Roullier are playing a ridiculous game where they each take turns throwing popping candy into the flames. An hour ago, they'd all returned from a school governors' board event and come straight here still dressed in their suits and rugby ties, each one delineating their specific rugby team status.

When I arrived at Wodebury from Lagos as an international student in Year Seven, the love and obsession with rugby was one of the many things I'd had to understand and acclimate to very quickly. Turns out that rugby is the sport of choice for elite boarding schools like this. There are the school rugby teams—one for each year, separated by gender—but it's the teams outside of school that are the most coveted. County, national, and, if you're talented enough, a Premiership Academy team, or the pinnacle, the England Academy team. If you get put forward by the school to try out for one of the latter two *and* you make it, you're practically deified.

Most of the current Year Twelve players wear red-striped ties, having been put forward for county back in Year Nine. But Marcus, the younger of the Villar twins, if only by minutes, is the only player among them in a gold-striped Premiership Academy team tie.

He's an amazing player, sure. But as I watch him now, I can't help but chuckle at the way everyone falls over the "cool and unflappable golden boy" rugby player persona he always puts on. To me, he'll always be my gushing shopping buddy on the holidays when Heather drags Luc and the Villars along with us.

But even for someone new to the sport and unfazed by his image, I'd understood how amazing the speed of Marcus's ascension through the ranks was. Now he's being eyed for the England Academy under-17s team, and if he wasn't so busy with all that, he'd probably be the school's Year Twelve boys' team captain too. But that position is held by his twin brother, Jordan, whose skills are second only to Marcus's. The twins were born in the summer, just weeks before the cutoff to end up in the year below. Considering how amazing they both are, I wonder if their team members wish they'd been born a few weeks later to avoid having to compete with them.

I turn my gaze to Jordan, and my smile fades. He's shifting uncomfortably where he sits with his casted foot up on the coffee table, tugging at his red-striped county tie. One of the other players has shifted their gameplay chatter to a discussion about ball dates, causing another round of jeers and laughter.

". . . because Marcus and Sarah are going together. Even Oliver Wei is going with Kitan. Where's your date, Jordan? You've been out for like a year, bro, and you haven't dated *anyone*," the player says, and pauses as everyone laughs again. "Maybe you can go with Luc here—he hasn't got a date either!"

The smile on Jordan's face is forced as Luc turns to him with an exaggerated somber expression. "Sorry, bro, I love you, but I don't like boys."

The group bursts into hysterics as Jordan shoves Luc into Marcus and the pair fall over each other.

Heather sits forward with a frown, frustrated by the interruption. "Shut up, guys, you're all so annoying."

"Thank you!" Jordan says, latching on to the easy exit. No one's going to ignore Heather. Not when her father is president of the governors' board and a top donor to the school's sports department, with an unspoken sway over who gets put forward for what team. "You're all just being annoying because I'm winning." Jordan throws another popping candy into the flames and the cheers of awe at the sparks send the conversation back to the game.

Heather turns to Sarah again, but my gaze stays focused on the group. With all eyes now diverted, Luc finally notices his friend's discomfort, holding his gaze in a silent question. Jordan just sends him a tired smile, gesturing for Luc to throw his candy, but Marcus intercepts Luc's toss.

"You idiot!" Luc says, his French accent thicker as he laughs, blond waves flying as he pushes Marcus off the sofa.

Unfazed, Marcus grins wide. "Next time, stay alert."

It's nice to see the three of them joking around. Jordan and Luc have been butting heads recently, with both of them going for the one national team position that just opened up. And Luc filling in as captain while Jordan's been injured has caused its own share of tensions. Before, you'd always see the three of them together, getting into mischief.

Sighing, I turn my attention back to Oliver's messages. Two more have come in since the one Heather interrupted.

Oliver

alright, i'll be there soon!

i'm outside

I don't waste another moment.

I slip on my wool coat, then grab my violin case from the sofa arm and rise to my feet. Heather and Sarah look up.

"I'm, umm, just going to practice with Oliver."

Heather rolls her eyes with a knowing smile and pulls out her phone. "Okay, we'll see you later then."

I exchange a quick look with Sarah while Heather's attention is averted, asking with my eyes if she's okay. She lifts her shoulder in a piti-ful shrug, but before I can silently inquire further, Sarah gestures with her chin for me to go on. *It's okay*, she mouths, and I nod in response.

I quickly cross the large room, the soft carpeted floor turning to sand-stone when I shut the heavy dark wood door behind me. The cold winter breeze almost makes me miss the uncomfortable heat from inside. But I ignore it, leaning back against the stone wall of the building. Closing my eyes, I take deep breaths and focus on letting go of the stifling feeling from the common room that had nothing to do with the temperature.

"You okay?"

Oliver.

The sight of him when I open my eyes, the cadence of his warm, rich tone, instantly does the job my deep breaths were trying to achieve. The tension in my shoulders falls away and my neutral expression gives way to a smile.

Standing there with his violin case clutched in his right hand, Oliver looks as perfect as always with his windswept waves, dark against his warm beige skin. I want to run my fingers through the longer strands that gently brush against his sharp jawline.

Instead, I smooth down my hair and take a little step forward. "Yeah, I'm fine."

"You sure? Because it's late, and you're already brilliant at this piece. *I'm* the one who needs more practice."

The breeze picks up a little more and my smile grows with it as I take another step toward him. His dark brown eyes widen for a second before they relax, and he smiles back, taking a step closer too. "Hi."

"Hey."

"You look—" He breathes out, tugging nervously at one of the silver hoops dangling from his ear. "You look so great."

My cheeks heat against the cold air, spreading down and all over. "You look so great too."

He reaches out tentatively and slips his warm fingers between mine, slowly bringing me closer to his side.

Holding hands. We've never done this before. I've never done this with anyone before.

He squeezes gently, and my hand responds automatically.

It's been a day since we were paired up at the matchmaking event and five months since we were chosen for this season's duet in orchestra. Before that, Oliver was always just "Sarah's cousin through marriage" who I only sort of knew because he was in orchestra too. But even when we started hanging out more after duet practice, him liking me never crossed my mind. That just never happens to me.

"We honestly don't have to practice today," Oliver whispers, squeezing my hand again. "You work so hard all the time already, and I just . . ."

He looks so genuinely concerned, a little crease between his brows, and my insides feel like the sparks of popping candy thrown into a flame.

A part of me wants to agree and take a break for the evening, but there's no room for error at Wodebury. Not for me. I may be the leader of the first violin section in the orchestra now, but I've seen how quickly this school can turn on you. The seasonal showcase is at the end of March, and even though I have my part of our duet down, I can always do *better*.

Plus, I just want to hang out with Oliver.

Grinning, I bump my shoulder with his gently. "It's okay, let's go."

His frown falls away to his usual easy smile, and we head off to the practice rooms.

The Bach piece is only about four minutes, but it's littered with complicated fingering and layered harmonies, so we spend almost an hour going over each section and repeatedly playing it through. My fingers glide over the taut strings, the sound traveling through my chin on the rest and expanding down my spine.

Looking away from the sheet music, I glance over at Oliver to find that he's already looking at me. We're coming up to our favorite part, just before the end, where the lively tempo builds.

A violin duet is like dancing together, finding the same rhythm while playing your own separate parts. But a violin duet with Oliver is like breathing as one, finding the same rhythm and staying there in sync.

Like always, the grins on our faces widen as the tempo climbs before it peaks, and we hold the final note. The music lingers in the air for a long moment, the sound interrupted only by our harmonized breaths as it bleeds into the gold vaulted ceiling and glossy warm wood floors of the practice room.

"It was perfect that time," Oliver whispers.

"It was," I say, matching his tone. "Done for the day?"

He nods. I rest my violin in the case, then move over to the mirror. I pull the band and bobby pins from the ponytail I'd packed my hair into to hold back the fringe, and then run through the loose waves of the wig to make sure the indents aren't too visible. The curtain fringe always gets in the way of my strings, but I generally avoid ponytails so I don't have to deal with the hassle of refreshing the curls. On days I know I'll be practicing, I usually pack my natural hair in a low bun instead. But this was an impromptu session after Oliver had texted me in a frenzy, and I was already planning to wash and restyle the wig tomorrow anyway.

He watches as I smooth down the strands, and when I'm done, we hold each other's gazes in the reflection. "Can I walk you back to Lady Chalford?"

"Sure."

We pack up our instruments and head outside with our fingers interlocked once more, leaving the tall Gothic structure of the music center behind.

I sneak glances at Oliver as we walk in comfortable silence through the back winter gardens with the leafless trees and crooked branches that sway in the breeze, casting lamplit shadows all around us. His usual soft smile plays on his lips, and his dark hair brushes along his cheekbones.

Oliver is always so at ease with himself, always so carefree, and I lean closer into him to welcome some of that energy by osmosis. "You know you're going to have to turn all the way back around to get to Roweton House, right?"

His smile turns to a smirk as he shrugs. "It's fine. This way we get to discuss how we're going to coordinate our outfits for the ball."

"Oh, are we?" I tease.

"I mean, if you want to. Not the whole thing, but maybe our accessories and stuff. I know you love fashion, and if you're anything like me, you already have your clothes sorted, right?" He raises a questioning brow, and I nod. "As expected, so it should be easy for us."

Us.

I squeeze his hand again, just because it's possible, and Oliver returns the gesture. "Okay, but I actually have two options. Old Hollywood fashion was fabulous, but I couldn't decide between a Lena Horne or Audrey Hepburn type of look. Iyanu already chose Dorothy Dandridge." I tuck a curl behind my ear. "Sarah and I planned to go shopping for our dresses together, but Mum and Dad were around for a short business trip that weekend."

Oliver snorts, somehow already knowing what's coming, and I nudge his side.

"Long story short, I was running late to have dinner with them before they left. Sarah couldn't find a dress and I couldn't decide between two dresses that I loved, so I sort of panic bought them both."

"Woman after my heart," he jokes, nose scrunching up with laughter, and *my* heart skips. "I sort of had the same situation too."

"Yeah?"

"Not quite as dramatic, but Dad loved one tux, Mum loved the other." He shrugs. "I'm probably going to end up with Mum's pick. She definitely has the superior eye for aesthetics. We'll just have to figure out how to let Dad down easy."

It's my turn to laugh.

He's right. As the founder and owner of a multinational marketing and advertising company, his mum's thing is definitely aesthetics. His family is Chinese Singaporean, so he spent his early years growing up in Singapore, but they relocated to London when it became the global headquarters for his mum's company. Plus, he and his mum have an extra-close bond; so much so that he didn't even have to tell her that he was bi, she just knew. Much like my mum, Oliver's always makes sure to call or video chat at least twice a week to check in, and on one such occasion I'd met Julia Wei. It was hard not to love her immediately.

Soon enough, Oliver and I turn toward the bridge over Lady Chalford's lake, and I'm reminded of the walks we'd started taking when we were done with practice. Or the spontaneous horse rides whenever we needed to de-stress and be mindless. Because much like then, Oliver launches into excited chatter, this time about his search for Old Hollywood actors.

"Whichever tux I go with though, I'm going to have to work hard to pull it off." And it's not said like he's fishing for a compliment, just in that charming way where he rarely takes himself too seriously.

"I'm pretty sure you'll be fine."

Grinning, Oliver continues as we cross the bridge over the lake. But when the massive redbrick walls of the Lady Chalford mansion come into view and we walk into my dorm block, he pauses. "I've just been going on and on, haven't I?" he asks sheepishly, pulling open the door to the stairwell.

I smile. "It's okay. I don't mind."

Oliver watches me for a moment, then nods. But he doesn't speak again until we get to my door. "Kitan?"

I pause midway through unlocking the door to turn back to him. His gaze is cautious, and the tension returns to my shoulders as my mind jumps to the worst conclusion.

This is where he says he doesn't actually want to go to the ball together.

It's ridiculous. He's said nothing to indicate it, but the reaction comes like second nature.

Oliver bites the corner of his lip. "Are you disappointed that we're going together?"

I blink once. Twice.

His expression grows even more concerned, hurt filling his eyes as the silence stretches on. "I just don't want you to feel like you *have* to go with me," he rushes out. "The matchmaking thing wasn't some binding contract. And like—"

"Wait." The word falls almost silently from my lips. "You're worried that *I* don't want to go with *you*?"

He drops his gaze to his pristine black boots.

By the end of a long round of questions and people being eliminated, Oliver had been left with two potential matches: me and another girl. Whenever more than one potential match made it to the end of a round, the contestant got to choose. And he'd chosen me.

Taking a deep breath, I step forward, lining up the front of my shoes with his. After a few moments, he lifts his gaze to mine, brown eyes softer, calmer.

"I want to go with you."

He must know that. I can't keep my emotions hidden around him.

"You sure?" he asks. "Because I'm not popular or whatever like the rugby guys. Marcus and the others. Hell, Luc and I have *never* gotten along. And I'm not like my cousin. Or, God forbid, Heather."

That makes me grin, even though it shouldn't.

"Those are your people," he continues, and I think about his people, the guys in orchestra that he'd made a fairly decent rock band with back in Year Eight. The complete opposite of the rugby guys. "You could go to the ball with any one of them."

I think about every time one of "them" used strategically worded questions to make sure I was eliminated from their round and they couldn't be matched with me. Over and over again, guys describing their ideal type with descriptors like "natural blonds" or "tan skin."

I think about the looks on the faces of the few guys who hesitated and then backtracked, deciding I wasn't worth it.

And yet they were all completely okay with Heather's new look.

I don't know if I'm flattered that Oliver thinks I could be with anyone, or disappointed that he didn't clue into what was happening last night. What always happens.

I sigh.

"Even if one of the guys did like me, they'd never ask me to go to the ball with them."

Oliver frowns, ready to protest, but something sparks in his gaze and he sobers. "I think I understand."

We're silent for a long moment, the look in his eyes reflecting the heavy feeling in my chest. Then he squeezes my hand again, still laced with his, and reaches out to take the other one, twining those fingers together too.

"I *really* wish it hadn't taken us getting paired up for this duet to finally talk to each other," I say.

He chuckles. "But at least it happened."

"Yeah."

I pause, wondering if I should continue.

This is Oliver.

I glance down at our shoes, before meeting his eyes again. "I *have* to be friends with all of them."

Oliver tilts his head. "*Have* to?"

I nod. "It's the only way I can . . ."

. . . not be on the outside like Iyanu.

I wonder for a second if Oliver misses being closer with Sarah like they used to be when they were at their old international school in Singapore. Their families spent a lot of time together because his mum and Sarah's stepmum are sisters; it was actually Oliver's mum's company opening their London office that got Sarah's stepmum on board with their own move back to England. But when they both started at Wodebury in Year Seven, they'd both found their own paths. Their own people.

I search my mind for the right words to explain, but Oliver seems to get it.

"I *want* to be your friend though."

His burst of laughter, a deep sound that seeps into my skin, is the best thing I've heard all day. "Oh no."

I can't help my grin. "You know what I mean."

Lifting our joined hands, he brushes my chin with his knuckle and the scent of his vanilla lotion fills my nostrils.

"Yeah, I do."

After a few minutes of silence and soaking in the delicate air in the tiny bubble of calm we've created, I finally find the strength to pull away.

My hands tingle from the absence of his.

"Tomorrow afternoon, do you maybe want to go riding?" Oliver asks.

In moments like these, it's hard not to wonder if he feels it too. That need to just be with each other all the time.

"I wish I could, but I've got Sunday dinner at Iyanu's house."

That's another thing I had to get used to when I started schooling here. Your Sunday afternoon meal is this whole affair with roasted potatoes, meat, gravy, stuffing, and Yorkshire pudding. And for some reason they call it Sunday dinner.

Oliver smacks his head lightly, and the sleeve of his coat falls down a little. I stare, slightly dazed, at the prominent veins along his toned arms. "Of course. Sorry I forgot. How about Monday after class?"

I'm nodding before he even finishes the sentence. "That sounds great. Stables at four thirty?"

"Perfect."

THREE

Kitan

Before applying to Wodebury, I went to one of the open days with Mum and Dad to have a look around. The tour guide, who'd explained to all the visiting prospectives that it was pronounced "Wood-bree," showed us around the school buildings, the vast grounds, and inside a few of the houses.

I'd immediately known I wanted to live in Lady Chalford. It was the closest house to the main Wodebury building and had spacious ensuite rooms with pretty light wood furniture and soft floral wallpaper. But the best part about it was the lake.

Schooling here was daunting but coming from an island with a view of a lagoon outside my bedroom window, the music from the lapping waters of Lady Chalford Lake was a welcome comfort. A familiar touchstone to nature, and the way it sings, no matter where you are. In the end I was lucky, because the room I was assigned was not only in Lady Chalford, but the dressing table sits in front of a large window that looks right out onto the water.

After untying the silk scarf around my edges, I check the hairline of my wig in the dressing table mirror, making sure the lace is laid and well blended, I run a hand down the back to confirm that the two short braids I'd pinned crisscross underneath the wig cap are still secure, before turning back to the view out the window.

The afternoon sunlight counteracts the chill of early February, which bodes well for my outfit choice for today's Sunday dinner at Iyanu's.

But will it be okay for our get-together with the rugby guys later this evening?

I tug at the collar of my tea dress, debating whether I should text Heather and ask.

Heather always knows the best way to go about things here. She always has—the perfect social butterfly navigating through any situation and turning them to her favor as easily as crossing a field of flowers.

In Year Nine history, before we were friends, I'd had to read a section from the textbook out loud in class. I can't even remember what the word I'd come across was, but apparently, I'd completely mispronounced it and the whole class burst into hysterics. As embarrassment crawled under my skin, all I could think about was all the other times something like that had happened. Mispronunciations, confusing turns of phrase, my "weird Nigerian colloquialisms" that "just aren't used here." I'd thought I was finally getting better at fitting in after two years.

And then somehow, Heather had magically flipped the room so everyone was laughing *with* me, before inviting me to join her and Sarah at their table for future classes.

No one's laughed at me since.

Yeah. Texting Heather it is.

But as I reach out for my phone, there's a knock at my door.

"Hey, Kitan." Sarah's voice comes muffled from the other side. "You still here?"

I grin. "Yup, it's open!"

I watch Sarah's reflection in the mirror as she walks in, hands behind her back with an overexaggerated sheepish expression on her face.

Turning around on the stool, I cross my arms with a faux stern expression. "What do you have behind your back?"

As Sarah perches down on the end of my bed, I catch sight of the silk material, and she quickly tucks it away.

I laugh. "All right, give it here. I still have some time before I have to leave."

Her eyes light up. "You're the best."

She hands me the blouse, and I grab a pair of tweezers from the dressing table drawer. "I'm sorry to ask again. I know you told me getting it was a bad idea for this exact reason."

I shrug. "It's fine. It's a cute blouse. And it looks great on you."

"Right?"

The stunning burgundy silk blouse has a pearl clasp in the back and zipper details on the shoulders. This, however, means that sometimes the seams get stuck in the zips. This is probably the tenth time I've had to sort it out for Sarah. But it's Sarah's favorite and she has no idea how to do it herself, so I'm happy to help.

"You know, Marcus was the one that taught me this trick," I say, gently prying the seam from each zipper with the tweezers. He'd learnt it to help his mum years ago, and he told me about it on one of our weekend shopping trips. "Maybe he'll give you all the fashion tips now that things are official."

Sarah's laughter in response is high and tinkling as she rolls her eyes. "Yeah, maybe."

They're an odd pair, but maybe they could be good together. Sarah and Marcus had been hanging out over the past few months and getting paired up at the matchmaking event seemed to be the catalyst for them to finally label things.

I pull out the last thread from the zip and trim the frayed edges with a pair of scissors. "Done."

Sarah turns from where she'd been inspecting my jewelry stand. "Yay! Thank you! I love you!"

She kisses my cheek as I hand over the blouse, then holds it up in front of the window, inspecting it happily.

"That for tonight at Roweton?" I ask, chuckling as I touch up the makeup on my cheek.

"Yup."

But the word comes out a little tired, her expression falling slightly.

I frown. "You okay?"

Sarah shrugs, folding the blouse in her lap as she settles down on the bed again.

"Yeah. I was just hoping to spend tonight getting ready for the week ahead. But now I can't afford to skip anything."

I'm about to ask what she means, but then it clicks. Head girl. Now that Heather's going for it too, she can't miss get-togethers like this. Not if she wants to keep up.

"I'm sorry about all that."

Sarah scrunches her lips to one side. "It's okay. You didn't know she'd do this. Neither of us thought she was actually being serious." She puts on a brave smile. "But it's okay. I spoke to my mum earlier and she gave me some more tips for the workshop. I'll figure something out."

Sarah has always been one of the most hardworking and determined people I know. It was the very first thing I noticed about her back in Year Seven, before we even became friends. Everyone could see it.

I poke gently at her knee. "Hey, if anyone can do it, it's you. You can pull this off. The teachers are bound to nominate you to run—they've seen all the years you've put into this. And when the time comes, people will vote you in, okay? Everyone loves you."

A tiny voice in the back of my head finishes the sentence, and Sarah's eyes echo the same.

But they all love Heather more.

Still, Sarah grins, bright and all the way to her eyes. "Thanks, Kitan. And for the blouse."

My heart warms. "'Course."

"All right," she says, heading to the door. "I'll let you get on."

After she leaves, I grab my phone and swiftly book a car, before gathering all my things in a purse and slipping on my peacoat. I hesitate, taking a quick glance back at the mirror to inspect my outfit again, then head out to the parking lot.

"Hey!"

I turn around to find Marcus approaching, fluffy curls blowing in the breeze and pearly whites bright with his wide smile. He's wearing a monochrome outfit: a black cashmere sweater and dress trousers under his wool coat, and smoky gray slip-ons.

Perfect for the get-together later.

"I was just talking about you," I say, elbowing his side as he joins me. "You just missed Sarah."

His light brown cheeks flush slightly. "Yeah? What about me?"

"I suppose that's for me to know," I tease.

He laughs. "Whatever, Ladipo. I'm meeting up with her later, so I'll just ask then."

I stick my tongue out at him.

"You headed to Sunday dinner?" Marcus asks.

"Yeah. Make sure you find some time for food too. I know you spent the morning on the pitch."

There's a slight discomfort in his eyes, but it doesn't last long as he shrugs. "Yeah, yeah, don't worry, that's where I'm headed. Quincy already ordered us pizzas."

In the distance the cab makes its way through the parking lot toward us, and Marcus notices it too. "Well, say hi to everyone for me!" he says, walking backward toward Brookfield. "And if you can sneak me back some leftover jollof that'd be great!"

I laugh. "Sure."

✳ ✳ ✳

After seeing Marcus's outfit, I'd sent a photo of mine to Heather as we drove to the Da Silva's, formulating a plan to leave Iyanu's early if I have to change.

The message had turned to "read" but Heather hasn't responded yet.

It'll be fine.

When we pull up outside the small duplex, I hop out the car with a thank you, still clutching my phone, and almost drop it when it buzzes.

Sunday 2:47 P.M.

Heather

> looks so great! i love that blush pink color on you, wish it looked that great on me!

The rush of excitement at the praise eases all my worry.

> let's try and get a photo together for my page later, yeah?

And the discomfort floods back in, bringing with it flashes of the reluctant photos I've already taken for her socials since she started her "new look."

Not now.

Taking a breath, I sift through my thoughts, sectioning away all the feelings that sting, before responding.

> thanks!

> it's pretty hectic today, but if we have time!

Aunty Dami always leaves the front door unlocked for me on Sundays, so I tuck my phone away and head into the house. Immediately, the delicious scent of Uncle Niyi's Sunday dinner fills my nostrils. The deep

33

smell of perfectly seasoned smoked meat with homemade gravy and roasted vegetables. That's the great thing about Sunday dinner: Uncle Niyi always throws a Nigerian spin on it, making sure everything is perfectly seasoned and including jollof and spicy gizdodo on the side.

I place my shoes on the rack by the entrance, then start up the hallway. The door to the living room is ajar, and there's a small hand poking out through the gap holding on to the outside handle.

Chuckling quietly, I join Feyi in the doorway.

She doesn't notice me at first, her eyes glued to the television that's playing the latest episode of our favorite Nigerian web series. She's dressed to leave the house, satchel hanging off one shoulder, clearly stopped midmotion during her exit. With the mathematics challenge and Olympiad training ramping up, she has to attend her gifted students study group for the next few Sundays.

Grinning, I wonder how many times she's stopped. If she's been traveling slowly from the loveseat to the arm of the chair to the back of it, and now the doorway.

Aunty Dami is sitting on the sofa, dark brown eyes also glued to the screen, and from what I remember, this week's cliff-hanger is just a few scenes away, so I better make my presence known now lest I ruin the build-up.

"Good afternoon, Aunty," I say, switching to my Yorùbá accent. The Da Silvas all speak with their regular accents or in Yorùbá at home, and it's always comforting to have this space where I can too.

Feyi jumps a little in surprise then smiles up at me, and I poke her dimpled cheek. "Hey, little one."

"Ahh, Kitan," Aunty Dami says, pausing the show. "Sho wà?"

Something deep rooted inside me settles, the way it always does. Another great thing about Sunday dinners: my name sounding the way it's supposed to. Pronounced correctly with a British accent is all right, but nothing beats the way it flows with that bass.

"I'm fine, Aunty. How are you?"

She hums, clapping her hands slowly. "This show o, where do I begin?"

I laugh. "I know, I watched it yesterday morning."

"So whose side are you on?" she asks, then lifts a hand before I can speak. "Just know that there's a right answer."

This time Feyi joins me in my laughter. "I'm telling you, Mummy, Kitan is going to be on my side."

I'm not sure whose side is whose, but I answer truthfully, pointing at the two men on the screen. "I understand where Gbemi is coming from, but I'm with Tolu on this one."

Feyi cheers, and Aunty Dami exclaims at the affront. "Gerrara here jọ!" she says, waving me out the door, and Feyi and I laugh harder. "You'll see, I'll be right in the end."

When we've all calmed down, I gesture over my shoulder. "Is Uncle Niyi in the kitchen? Let me greet him."

"Yes, and Iyanu is upstairs."

My smile dims a little, but I nod. "Okay."

Before I turn to leave though, Aunty Dami speaks again, eyes wide in remembrance. "Oh! Let me tell you now before I forget. I bought Indomie when I was in London, so you can take it back to the dorms with you. Pepper soup flavor. They're in the store."

I clasp my hands together gratefully. "Thank you so much. I was running low."

Aside from late night garri with sugar, water, and ice (regardless of the weather), access to late night noodles you can throw in the microwave are a must as a boarder, and the perfection that is Indomie is the best homesick meal. When I go back to Lagos between terms, I always designate a section of one of the suitcases to bring back chicken flavor, green Indomie, and my favorite: pepper soup flavor. Whether I have it with hard-boiled eggs, dodo, or my stash of frozen suya, Indomie is a saving grace.

Especially as someone who's often homesick and regularly needs refills during term time.

As I head toward the kitchen, Feyi follows behind me. "You okay?" I ask her.

She nods. "Just wanted to say thank you. I got full marks on my music homework."

The warmth in her eyes widens my smile. "That's awesome, I'm glad it worked out," I say, then tap gently on her temple. "I'm not surprised though. You've got a great head for maths, which can sometimes be half the journey with music, so that gives you an edge."

Feyi giggles, but whatever she's about to say next is interrupted by an alarm going off on her phone. She quickly turns it off, glancing forlornly over her shoulder at the living room door. "The study session shuttle will be here in five . . . I'll have to finish the episode when I get back."

"You'll love it."

I watch as she quickly slips on her shoes at the door and heads out, before making my way into the kitchen.

FOUR

Iyanu

Sunday dinner is awkward.

Which, fair enough, it always is. But Feyi, the usual buffer that keeps our parents from noticing that Kitan and I aren't *actually* saying any words to each other, is at her gifted students study group.

And so the conversation as we eat is characterized by my slightly delayed "hmms" and "ahhs" of participation between Kitan's overly smiley responses to Mum and Dad's questions. ("I hope you're not over-extending yourself at orchestra practice, dear?" "Oh no! The piece is great!" "Any requests for dessert next week?" "Sorry, I can't make it! The rugby team has an Away game, but Marcus says hello.")

It's hardly my fault. My mind is too focused on how I'm going to broach "The Heather Situation" with Kitan without it turning into an argument.

When the meal finally ends, Kitan offers to do the dishes, and I head to the bathroom (not stalling) before returning to the scene of the, hopefully, no crime. The kitchen sink is right opposite the door, and Kitan tenses the moment I walk in even though she stands with her back to it. Somehow, she knows I'm the person behind her, and she's already on edge.

But before I can start my speech, I spot Kitan's phone unlocked on the dining table.

The lower part of the screen has little soapy fingerprints on it, so she must have quickly turned around to unlock and reply to the message currently displayed.

Sunday 4:46 P.M.

Heather

> Sarah's gone and lost her pearl necklace, she says she thinks someone stole it, so we're all gonna wear our Tiffany's necklaces on Tuesday instead of Thursday

> sure! sounds like a great plan!

The message from Heather is unsurprising. She always makes the three of them coordinate their outfits. But what's more annoying is Kitan's deferential response.

I clear my throat, trying not to grit my teeth when Kitan sighs. She shuts off the tap and turns around, grabbing a dish towel to dry her hands. Over her perfectly pressed linen tea dress is Dad's favorite teal apron. She always dresses up for Sunday dinner. She dresses up all the time. Like flawless fashionable armor. The last time I saw her in leggings and a slouchy jumper, like my outfit today, was long before we stopped speaking. But she usually seems confident in her ensembles, and right now, with the way she tugs on her Peter Pan collar, all I can see is discomfort. And it's hard to pinpoint why.

She clearly doesn't want to have a conversation, but that sentiment usually manifests itself as an aloof stare. I settle down in one of the dining chairs, a calculated choice that'll hopefully help her feel like this isn't some kind of attack.

"I wanted to talk to you about something."

"Sure. What's up?"

Kitan's voice is always so delicate and soft. It's been that way since we were kids. Gentle. Even when she's angry or upset.

"It's about Heather."

She tenses up a little more, and I hold in my sigh. No matter how delicately I'd tried to say the words, my disdain for Heather still bled through.

"What are we going to do about this whole blackfishing thing?"

There's a long silence as Kitan stares down at the dish towel, twisting it between her fingers.

"Nothing."

Her response is exactly what I'd expected, but I still feel a twinge of disappointment. "Well, she won't listen to me, the school definitely won't do anything about it, and her devoted followers on her socials clearly don't care." I shift in my seat. "So I thought maybe a gentle word from a friend might get her to stop. We don't want things to get worse."

I doubt that Kitan saying something will help, but it's worth a shot.

Kitan looks away, scanning the walls around the small kitchen before turning back to me.

"I don't think there's anything I can say," she whispers.

For a split second, I think I see a tiredness in her eyes, a heavy kind of vulnerability, but then it disappears.

And there it is. The aloof facade.

It's hard not to think about the first time this happened. Kitan deferring to Heather. It was Year Nine, a few weeks after Heather moved here because her dad was made president of the school's governors' board. In barely a month, she'd somehow become the most popular person at Wodebury.

I'd initially thought Heather and I could be friends—she was just really charming that way. But then we ended up on the Year Nine student council and disagreed on *everything*. Whenever I proposed a change, she pushed back.

Heather and Kitan, along with Sarah, were in a lot of the same classes, so they were more friendly than I'd realized, because it all came to a head in a student council meeting. I can't remember the exact argument that day, but Kitan had said, "I'm sure Heather didn't mean anything by it," and that was the beginning of the end. We started distancing ourselves from each other: no longer hanging out between classes, then outside school, where we became politely reserved at Sunday dinners. And by the end of Heather's sixth week at Wodebury . . . we were done. There was no reaching back, not even after everything else that followed during that year.

"You don't think there's anything you can say."

Kitan bites her lip, another split-second motion that instantly disappears. "I'm not like you, Iyanu."

The fact that *those* were the words she chose to say makes anger suddenly spike in my veins. I clench at the edge of my seat, taking a deep breath before meeting her eyes again. "Really? And what am I like?"

"You can't"—she fumbles around for the word—"compartmentalize. I can. It's the only way I—" She cuts herself off, staring down at her feet, and another long silence descends.

Compartmentalize.

It's an interesting way of putting it. And it hurts. For a lot of reasons. "Right."

Then a series of short buzzes interrupts whatever Kitan was going to say, and our eyes dart to her phone on the table. I watch as she types out a response to the messages that, from her expression, seem to be from Heather.

After a few messages back and forth, she slides her phone into the front pocket of the small leather bag she'd paired with today's outfit and meets my eyes again. "I'm sorry, I have to get back."

"What?" I fumble for a way to recapture the conversation, but after swiftly taking off Dad's apron, Kitan slips the bag onto the crook of her arm and hurries out the door.

She nearly collides with Feyi, who must have just been dropped off by her friend's mum.

"Bye, Kitan!" Feyi shouts to her retreating form, and Kitan smiles back over her shoulder before quickly heading out the front door.

Then Feyi turns to me, her smile fading at the look on my face. "Nunu, what's wrong?"

"Don't worry, it's nothing," I respond, resolving to figure out a way to speak to Kitan tomorrow.

"Nunu?"

Feyi's hesitant voice from the other side of my bedroom door the next morning pulls me from my search for my missing right Doc, and I shuffle out from under my bed.

"I know, lovely." I breathe out, giving my room yet another once over before diving to check under the dressing table again. "I'm coming. If we leave in the next ten minutes, we'll still be on time for school."

I rifle behind the stacks of old negative binders, hoping that this time the other shoe will miraculously appear there.

It doesn't.

I slide back out from under the dressing table and slump down onto my fluffy center rug.

It's not that my room is messy. In fact, I know exactly where everything is—bed, dressing table, camera gear, bookcase, record player, easel. But there's just a lot of stuff and not enough space. So sometimes, usually after someone goes around with the vacuum, things get lost in the cracks. I'd saved up a good fraction of my earnings working every day this past summer at the old bookshop in town to be able to afford those low-rise Docs. They can't be missing.

The start of Year Twelve meant no more school uniform, which meant that the upkeep of being at Wodebury significantly increased. I needed "better" clothes. In the end, it took a strategic day trip to different secondhand shops in the wealthy areas in London, to find said better clothes without destroying my bank account. I was very lucky to head home that evening with a herringbone blazer, a slightly worn but good quality wool coat, and a handful of turtleneck sweaters. Everything else was supplemented by the sales racks in various high street shops, and Mum making me a couple of tapered trousers with decent quality fabric we'd found for cheap on Petticoat Lane.

Sighing, I drag myself on all fours over to the my plug beside the record player Dad and I share where my phone is charging, deciding to ask if he or Mum have seen the right shoe before giving up and wearing loafers instead.

Feyi knocks again. "Nunu, I'm sorry."

There's an unsteady hitch to her voice, and all thoughts of footwear disappear.

Stumbling to my feet, I yank open the door.

Feyi stands there in her pristine Wodebury uniform: a white button-up with a floppy navy bow tie, Wodebury gray blazer and jumper, and a navy and gray tartan skirt. But her hair is . . .

"What happened?" I ask, dropping to my knees in front of the teary twelve-year-old. "Didn't Daddy do your hair yesterday?"

Dad had spammed the family group chat with photos of his latest creation.

But now, instead of intricately designed cornrows tied back into a puff at the nape of Feyi's neck, what was once a thick, coily cloud of 4c hair at the back is strangled into what was presumably supposed to be two long plaits—but she only succeeded in tangling her hair.

She shrugs hopelessly, her bottom lip wobbly. "I—I don't want it out in the back."

Cupping her warm cheeks, I wipe her tears with the pads of my thumbs. "Did you tell Daddy that?" I ask.

Her watery eyes meet mine and she shrugs again. "He was having fun." Combined with the pitiful motion, her words almost have me crying too. "A-And I didn't mind it yesterday," she continues. "I liked it."

I think about her wide smiling face in the photos.

"But you don't like it anymore?"

Feyi doesn't say anything for a few seconds, a deep crease between her brows as she thinks, and then she's crying heavily again.

I pull her tightly into my chest, cradling her head in the space between my neck and shoulder. "It's okay, lovely. We all have bad hair days," I say, rubbing her back gently.

When Feyi isn't being a little know-it-all (deservedly so, considering she's a literal genius), she can be pretty sensitive sometimes. It's one of the things I love most about her—she has the greatest capacity for love and empathy of anyone I've ever known. But her emotions can overwhelm her sometimes.

This though, this feels a little different.

Her sobs fade to tiny sniffles as she prepares to speak again, and I resolve to listen extra closely so I can get to the bottom of this.

"I just wanted to try it myself, but it wouldn't work!" she says, hiccuping loudly into my ear, but I just squeeze her tighter. "I was going to ask Mummy, but she got called into the hospital early this morning, and Daddy has already gone to the gallery."

Ah.

Feyi had needed something done, so she'd taught her mind how to do it, but when she'd tried to do the same for her hands, she'd hit a wall. This happens sometimes with Feyi, though it's rare, because she's good at pretty much everything she sets her mind to. I can only imagine how frustrating it would be to have a brain that's always moving at light speed, and a regular human body that's always trying to keep up.

I pull back, ushering her into my dressing table chair. "Okay, let me sort this out." I roll up the sleeves of my beige turtleneck sweater, then quickly grab a bottle of detangling leave-in conditioner and a wide tooth comb from the bathroom and set them down on the dressing table in front of the mirror. Feyi's face is wet and snotty, so I grab a packet of baby wipes from the top drawer and hand it to her. "Here, clean yourself up, okay? Then you can cream your face again," I say, gesturing to a bottle of lotion.

She nods a little, still sniffling, but gets to work.

After coating some conditioner on my fingers, I begin the long process of detangling.

We're going to be so late.

After a few minutes of working, I realize that I can salvage the cornrows since not much damage had been done there and settle on simply redoing the two long plaits at the back. "I'll teach you how to do these, okay? On Wednesday since we have a half day."

Her dark brown eyes, so like mine, light up, and my heart brightens. "Yeah, you sure?" she asks. "I was gonna ask Daddy, but he's had that new shipment come in for the gallery, so his hours are all weird."

Feyi is definitely past old enough to be doing her own hair, to really understand the labor of love it takes. But as the younger sibling, well, let's just say eldest Black girls learn to take care of everything much earlier. Besides, Feyi spent all that free time being a science prodigy, so I guess it's okay.

And it's never too late to learn.

I grin. "I'm sure."

"And how to straighten it too?"

My smile falters a little. We've never straightened her hair. Mum threw out relaxers in favor of her healthy type 4 natural coils back when I was born, determined to break the cycle of damage imposed by white beauty standards. So, just like she did with me, Feyi's thick coils have been left untouched by intense heat and alterations for as long as possible—healthy, happy hair, "as fresh as the day she was born" until she was old enough to choose how she wanted to style it.

Well, she's past old enough now.

I poke the side of her neck and she swats me away with a snort.

"Sure, if that's what you want."

She nods excitedly and I have to hold her head steady again before I can continue.

"Thanks, Iyanu."

I work silently for a few minutes before Feyi speaks again. "Have you started writing the *WeCreate* article yet?"

A rush of terrified excitement skitters up my spine. I'd introduced Feyi to *WeCreate* magazine a few years ago and she'd adored it. "Not yet. But it isn't due until like noon on the fifteenth, so I still have a little under two weeks? Yeah, twelve days." I pause, securing the end of the first braid with beads and a rubber band before moving to detangle the next half. "The film's already developed, I just need to print out my favorites. I left my stuff in there on Saturday, so everything is sorted and ready to go for today. Once I see how the pictures turned out, I'll know what I want to write."

Feyi winces a little as I loosen a particularly stubborn knot. "I wish I could have come with you to the fair."

I wish she could have too. Living where we do, God knows it was ages before I got the chance to really see, much less be completely surrounded by people who look like me. The Black Girls Winter Fair was exactly that. And now I'd have that feeling to keep for myself and relive over and over again through the photos I'd taken. But that weekend had just been too busy for Feyi with the Astrophysics Expo she'd had to attend.

"I know, lovely. I wish you could've come too."

But she just smiles. "It's all right. I'll read all about it when you're done writing the article."

Grinning, I brush back her baby hairs with a toothbrush. "You'll be the first one I send it to."

By the time I'm done with Feyi's hair, it looks leagues better than my three-day-old twist out I'd decided to pack into a low bun, and we're only fifteen minutes behind schedule. "All right, go grab your satchel. If we get going now, we'll only miss form time," I say, shoving on my loafers. "You know my car always takes ages to start."

We'd gotten this older model secondhand, but if I get this *WeCreate* job, then I can save up for another before it completely packs in on me. Which really can't happen. We have only one other car and Mum uses it while Dad cycles to work. Feyi and I will have no secure way to school with how wild Mum's hospital schedule is, and the buses here are notoriously unreliable.

Feyi jumps to her feet, ready to rush from the room, but pauses mid-motion. "Ermm, Nunu? Why is your shoe on the windowsill?"

I glance over, and sure enough, the right foot of my black leather Docs is shoved between the window and a tall pile of fiction paperbacks.

We spend only two minutes in hysterics before grabbing our satchels and rushing outside.

FIVE

Iyanu

When we arrive at school, Feyi hurries out the car the second the usual angry groan of the vehicle stops, determined to catch the last few minutes of form time. But I have a free first period, so I head toward Wodebury House to sign in and get an early start on prep in the darkroom.

As I cross the main courtyard, heading toward the Sixth Form office to sign in, a tall guy comes bursting out the door. His eyes breeze past me and then he does a double take. "Not cool, Da Silva. Not cool." He shoves past me, the rugby bag over his shoulder knocking hard into mine.

I'm too shocked by the venom in his words to say anything as I grab my throbbing joint, but by the time I gather my wits he's already disappeared out of the courtyard.

What the hell.

I head into the office, only slightly irritated by the cheery "Welcome!" sign embossed on the wood-paneled walls above the front desk.

"Morning, Mrs. Keane," I say, doing my best to smile at the blond receptionist as she comes out of the printer room. Her smile in return is bright against her pale white skin. She hands me the sign-in clipboard for Year Twelves, and I'm glad for my efforts.

"Good morning, Iyanu. I didn't expect to see you today. I thought it was only when you have two frees in the morning that you don't attend form?"

I shrug, instantly regretting it as my shoulder twinges.

"You're right, Miss. But there was a bit of a hair crisis this morning with Feyi."

Mrs. Keane chuckles, gesturing to her slightly disheveled bun. "Seems I'm not alone then."

I start to sign my name as she heads back into the printer room, and it's only then that I register the prickling stares on the back of my neck.

Sitting on the chesterfield sofas in the waiting area are three girls huddled around the middle one's phone, whispering to each other. Every few seconds they steal glances at me as they laugh at whatever is on the screen.

An uncomfortable heat creeps up my spine and I grit my teeth to keep from saying anything. They're probably in the year below, the relaxed state of their uniforms giving off that "this is the last year we'll have to wear this" vibe. But that doesn't mean I can't glare at them, and after a few moments, they finally notice that I've noticed them, and try to pretend to be doing something else.

Rolling my eyes, I storm out of the office to their eruption of laughter.

Seriously, what the hell is going on?

It's not completely odd. When you move through this town, this world, in my skin, someone's always watching. But this feels different. Here on the grounds of Wodebury Hall, me and my camera move under the radar. If I'm invisible to my own peers, why the hell are some Year Elevens texting about me? Why did that random rugby lad pay me any mind?

I shove a hand into my coat pocket to grab my phone and ask Navin what I missed.

A jolt of fear pierces through my chest as I come up empty. I check my other coat pocket, my trousers, every corner and crease of my satchel, *my socks*. But the battered black device is nowhere, and the fear sends my heart into a frenzy.

Is that what this is about? Did someone steal my phone?

My lungs squeeze tight.

There's nothing particularly wrong on my phone, but you never know what someone could do. Who they could text, what they could post.

Just as the hyperventilation begins, I remember.

In the general disorder of this morning, I'd left my phone charging at home.

Blowing out a breath, I scrub my hands down my face, digging my index fingers into the corners of my eyes.

It takes a few minutes to get my respiratory system back in proper functioning order, but once I do, I quickly cross the courtyard again to Wodebury House. The grand atrium has a high ceiling with classic pink marble columns around the circular space, and floral Greek motifs carved into the walls above them. As always, my hurried footsteps echo off the marble floors, the atrium empty aside from the busts of random dead white people in the alcoves between the columns. Their blank stares seem to follow me as I make my way to the art department.

Okay. Locker first for my books, and then darkroom.

The long hallway always smells faintly of turpentine and oil paints, and as I welcome the comforting scents of my second home, my nerves slowly start to ease. The right side of the hallway is lined with dark wood classroom doors interrupted periodically by a set of Wodebury-gray two-tier lockers. Old wrought-iron French doors with ivy growing through the twisting design line the stone walls on the left side, leading to a small central garden, and the soft sunlight filtering through waiting rain clouds highlights my steps along the way.

Just as I make it past the second set of lockers, the trill of the first bell cues the loud scraping of chairs and rumbling chatter from behind the classroom doors.

And then it's mayhem.

Students burst out into the hallway, hundreds of voices crashing against one another, screams and laughter bouncing off the walls. I try to shove my way through the mob to my locker at the end of the corridor, already sweating beneath my turtleneck as I maneuver through pockets of people shouting, arguing . . . *crying*?

I look around hurriedly, and my heart starts to speed up again.

This isn't just the general rowdiness of people going to their first classes.

This is genuine chaos.

Two guys burst out of a classroom, grabbing at each other's throats, and the metallic bang as they slam into a set of lockers grates against my ears.

I hurry forward, ducking to narrowly avoid a flying water bottle, only to stumble past a group of girls shouting at each other, brandishing what looks like . . . Polaroids?

Through the French doors, I can see across the small garden into the hallway on the other side to find similar chaos.

What the hell? Is this happening everywhere?

And then to my left, a blond guy whispering to the group around him points right at me.

Suddenly, like a game of telephone, whispers travel down the hallway. Everyone who isn't in some sort of confrontation turns in my direction. For a moment, I'm back in Year Nine in the days before my falling-out with Quincy.

I clutch tightly at my satchel strap, but the words and whispers skitter along my arms, slivered eyes stalking me as I hunch in on myself and pick up my pace.

". . . it's her . . ."

". . . can't believe she would . . ."

My fingers itch for my camera, deep regret weighing in my stomach at having left it with my negative binder in the darkroom on Saturday. It probably couldn't do anything now, but every cell in my body yearns for the anonymity of hiding behind it.

And then I catch the sound of my name from somewhere to my right.

". . . Iyanu. Like why even do this?"

The girls talking haven't noticed me yet, but I recognize their faces from Year Twelve assemblies. Before I can hurry on, the blonde catches my eye, and the poison in her gaze nearly melts the skin off my face as I freeze in place. There's no telling how long she glares at me, but it can't be more than a few seconds before she turns and whispers something to the girl next to her. The brunette glances up from what they'd been looking at, another Polaroid, and then hurriedly begins typing on her phone.

I jolt back into motion, practically running to the end of the hallway.

With the photography lab at the end of the corridor around the next corner, I rustle quickly through my satchel for my locker key and shove it into the lock. It takes a few tries, every eye in the hallway drilling into the back of my skull making my hands tremble, but I finally get it open.

I shove my head into the locker, desperate for some respite. And then I feel a presence behind me.

"Iyanu?"

I turn with a jerk.

Quincy stands there, large form highlighted by the soft glow of the light behind him. Hesitantly, he moves closer, and the motion does no favors for the beating in my chest.

Much like how I did Feyi's hair this morning, his thick curls are braided in two long plaits that curl behind his ears, enhancing the clean line of his undercut.

"Quincy, hey."

My voice is surprisingly steady considering the frenzy of my mind.

"H-Hey."

The crack in his voice gives me pause. It's been a long time since I've heard uncertainty in Quincy's tone. His skills on the rugby field led to popularity at Wodebury, and that pulled the once bashful boy out of his shell. And even though it eventually meant the demise of "the dynamic duo" as the years went by, it was nice to see the cheeky confidence he'd only ever had with me come effortlessly around others.

But now, as he stands here, it's like a regression. There's caution in his darting eyes, and he keeps tugging periodically at the hem of his navy blazer.

We stand in silence for a few moments, and just as I decide to ask him what on earth is going on, his eyes finally settle on mine.

"You . . . like me?"

I choke on air.

His voice lilts a little on the *l* like it occasionally does when he's excited or uneasy, teasing at the light Cuban accent that used to be much stronger when we were younger.

"What?"

I hold on to the locker door to keep upright.

"You like me?"

Oh my God.

I glance up the corridor to find pretty much everyone watching us, then turn back to him.

Of the three Villar brothers, I've always thought that Quincy was the most beautiful. Perhaps I'm biased because we used to be best friends, but most people at school would disagree, fawning over the twins' identical dimpled smiles and high cheekbones. It's not that they don't think Quincy's attractive too—his round at the matchmaking event was proof enough of that. It's just that he doesn't look anything like his brothers, with his darker brown skin and lightly bearded face.

I scan said face, looking for answers, for *anything*, because I've never said any of this out loud. And despite how it might seem, it's all become so matter-of-fact that I barely think about it anymore, much less feel the need to act on it.

Definitely not.

Quincy shuffles on his feet again. "Is it true?"

His expression is mostly unreadable, but the confusion I detect is the same one that's stiffened my limbs, poking at the painful history that lingers between us.

Panicked, I focus instead on Quincy's next words.

"Is it true?" he asks, more confidently this time, and I almost shiver at the undecipherable tone hiding underneath. "Because if it's true, I mean, I know we haven't been best friends since we were like fourteen, but I thought we were cool now? You could have told me in person. I would have liked to know—"

"I don't like you."

His mouth snaps shut at my sudden declaration, and my face heats as I register what I've just said.

I scramble for what to say to end the silence, but I can't think of anything. After a few horrifying seconds, Quincy's gaze drops down to his Oxfords, severing our intense stare down.

"Oh."

This seems to snap my brain into gear.

"I mean I like you, but I don't *like* you. Like, not like that. You're great—"

It's my turn to snap my mouth shut, but as I dart my eyes to my feet, I freeze at the sight of what's in his hand.

There between Quincy's fingers is a Polaroid, just like the ones that I'd seen those girls holding. He must have pulled it out from somewhere during our exchange.

I focus on the image with a frown.

It's the photo I took of him at the matchmaking event.

This is what tips my heart into cardiac arrest zone, even as my bewilderment deepens. The fact that he even has this photo.

"Where did you get that?" I croak out.

"From you?" he asks, and the confused crease between his brows is so deep now that they form one continuous line.

I ignore how adorable the expression is and take the offending item as he hands it to me.

Anger bristles deep in my stomach.

I just took this photo on Friday. The images from the matchmaking event are all hanging up in the darkroom right now. Which means that someone must have scanned it and printed it out as a Polaroid.

Trying to understand, to piece it together and make it all make sense, I flip the Polaroid over.

Written in black ink is a message that has me bracing against the lockers.

Iyanu has a crush on you.

It's so . . . juvenile. So obviously untrue. Yes. Definitely untrue.

And yet the tell-tale burning starts behind my eyes.

"What is this?" I whisper, meeting Quincy's gaze again.

He flounders. "The photos you took on Friday? A bunch of us from the matchmaking event got one. They have messages on them. Secrets about everyone." He pauses, pulling out another Polaroid from his pocket and handing it to me. "You didn't send them out?"

The second photo is the one I'd reluctantly taken of Heather, Kitan, and Sarah.

I quickly turn it over.

Quincy wants to go with Iyanu.
Heather is just a pity date.

My stomach turns.

"Who got this one?" I ask, even though the worst possible name is screaming in my brain.

"Heather." Quincy shifts on his feet. "We're not going to the ball together anymore."

"Oh my God, she broke it off?"

Quincy thinks for a moment, like he's doing a quick calculation in his mind, and I squeeze my eyes shut, resting my forehead against the lockers.

I cannot deal with an attack from Heather right now.

"Did you not send these out? It's not true?"

But I'm barely listening to Quincy now, my thoughts circling back through our conversation, and this time it clicks.

A bunch of people got one.

"How many?" I ask, eyes snapping open again as I think about how many photos I took that evening.

Quincy sighs. "I dunno. A lot of us who were there on Friday got a Polaroid with secrets and stuff written on the back. But they spread around and now everyone knows—"

I break out into a run, not caring if Quincy follows, and hurry around the corner.

I burst into the empty photography lab and weave through the desks, banging my elbows and hips on the corners in my haste to get to the darkroom at the back of the classroom. Just before I reach the entrance, I notice a ruined pile of cut up photo paper by the scanner.

No no no no no.

After scrambling through the revolving doors, I skid to a halt at the state of the dimly lit room before me.

Someone has clearly been in here since I left on Saturday.

All my hanging photos are gone. Whoever had taken them tried to clean up after themselves, but one of the lines had come unattached and hung limply down the wall next to the cubbies.

A distant part of my brain registers Quincy coming in behind me, but I'm more focused on the cubbies.

Slowly moving toward them, I stuff the Polaroids from Quincy in my pocket, heart squeezing tighter with each step.

I grab my camera bag first.

The camera is still in there, safe and secure, but I barely have time to rejoice because that's the only thing in the cubby.

I search it again, then dart hastily around the room, eyes sweeping over every corner and crevice.

My binder full of negatives is gone.

Including the ones from the Black Girls Winter Fair.

There's no telling how long I sit there crying on the floor of the darkroom, but at some point, Quincy disappears.

"Iyanu, oh my God, you better be in here."

Navin's distant voice arrives before he does, stumbling through the lab.

"Why haven't you been answering my texts? *Quincy* told me where you were. What's that about?"

A loud crash echoes into the darkroom, followed by a whispered "oops" before Navin carries on, his voice closer this time.

"It's actually a hellscape out there. Who the hell wrote all that stuff on your—"

His voice cuts off as he walks into the darkroom, spotting me huddled in the corner against the wall.

I can barely see him through the glaze of tears.

"Oh, babe." He hurries over and wraps me up in his arms. "Who did this?"

A tiny part of me goes soft with the reassurance that, unlike everyone else, Navin knows it wasn't me who did this. The larger part just wants to run away. It's barely midmorning and I already have a throbbing shoulder to show for this mess; there's no telling what's still left to come.

I stuff my face in the crook of Navin's neck. "It wasn't me."

He wraps his arms tighter around me, smoothing a gentle hand over my hair comfortingly.

"I know it wasn't, love. You know what it feels like to be on the other end of a rumor; you wouldn't do this."

The words smart, setting off the usual ache of memories, but I don't let them consume me.

Then there's a rustling sound, and out of my periphery Navin pulls out another Polaroid, holding it out to me. "And there's this . . ."

It's a photo of him laughing, one of my favorites from Friday.

Wiping harshly at my eyes, I take the Polaroid from him and flip it over.

Jordan thinks you're the hottest guy in our year.

Navin chuckles softly at my incredulous expression.

"If you knew Jordan liked me back, you would've just told me."

I laugh wetly. "Yeah."

My voice is so wobbly that I barely recognize it, but I welcome the sliver of joy that Navin's presence always brings, and we sit in silence, the gentle buzz of the safe lights above us soothing in its familiarity.

"How did this happen?"

Navin sighs.

"Whoever released the Polaroids left them on the tables during form time. A bunch of Year Twelves who were at the matchmaking event got them. So, as folks trickled into form, they took photos of the Polaroids, sent them around, and well, they spread like wildfire. Pretty much everyone's seen them by now." He pauses, contemplating. "The messages were all kinds of things about everyone. Their relationships, friendships, themselves. And if they're true . . ."

He looks a little impressed, and for a moment I catch a glimpse of what the old Navin before Wodebury might have been like. It's kind of hard to believe now that the sweetest person I know, and my only real friend, was always "in the know" at his old boarding school. Always made sure to be in the center and stay on top of the social scene by spinning every secret to his advantage. Bad choices he made to overcompensate and fit in.

But people change. He worked on himself and was brave about it. And change he certainly did. You can't get any further from the center than here on the fringes with me.

"Back at my old school, only the people at the top would know these kinds of secrets. Because if you want to stay there, you have to know everything. Not just anyone can get this kind of information about people, much less secrets about the people who've made it their business to run things." Then he smirks, nudging my side. "Which is another reason why I know it wasn't you."

I let out another wet chuckle, but sober again at the way his expression changes. "But it's probably all lies anyway. Mine certainly is."

"You never know," I whisper.

But he just shrugs and pulls out some wet wipes from the emergency kit in his bag, then begins wiping the tears from my face. The tender strokes gently soothe my heated skin.

"Some of them *are* definitely lies though," I say, pulling out the Polaroids I got from Quincy. "Look. This was Quincy's."

Another smirk slowly creeps across Navin's face as he reads the message. "'Iyanu has a crush on you.'" He raises an eyebrow. "Are you sure this one's a lie?"

A weird feeling settles in my stomach, a fluttering that's quickly replaced with dread as the memories start to creep forward again.

Navin transferred to Wodebury in Year Nine, which meant that he came into my life just before Quincy left it, so he was there for the fallout. We'd met at one of the school's queer society events. Jordan, who was still in the closet at the time claimed to be at the event "just to help

58

out." Quincy and I were both working the bi information table, and when Quincy left the booth, Navin had sidled up to me, gay men's pride flag pinned to his lapel, teasing that I couldn't stop staring at Quincy. I'd teased back that he was doing the same with Jordan, and the rest was history.

I scoff. "I don't have a crush on Quincy. What are we? Seven?"

That just makes Navin's smirk grow. "If you say so."

"Stop it," I whine, nudging him, and he giggles, making a zipping lips motion before setting back to his task of cleaning my face.

He grabs some lotion from the emergency kit, taking extra care underneath my eyes as he rubs it gently into my skin.

"Everyone really thinks it was me?"

He nods solemnly. "Yeah. You were the one taking the photos on Friday. And there wasn't a Polaroid for you in form. They've put two and two together and gotten eighteen, I guess."

I sigh. "Okay."

Appraising my face, Navin nods once, then puts the lotion away, deeming me presentable again. "Done," he says, poking my cheek.

Feeling much more like myself again, I pour all the gratitude I can into my eyes. "I love you."

"I love you too."

He pulls me into his arms again and I wince a little as his shoulder jostles mine.

I let out another sigh at his questioning look. "Some rugby dude bumped into me. I'm guessing the Polaroids messed up his life or whatever."

"Sorry, babe."

We settle back against the wall and I'm fully ready to stay here cuddled into Navin's side for the rest of forever, but as I glance back over at my camera on the table, my mood darkens again.

"They took my photos."

"Huh?"

"Whoever sent the Polaroids out stole *all* my photos. The ones from the matchmaking event that were hanging to dry, yes, but they also stole my negative binder."

I see exactly when the realization sparks in Navin's dark brown eyes, the anger burning through me igniting in him.

"The photos from the Black Girls Winter Fair for *WeCreate*."

"Yes."

But the rest of my response is interrupted by the soft chime of Navin's phone.

A flurry of emotions cross his face as he reads the texts.

"What is it?"

He looks up with a sigh, tucking the phone away.

"Heather has called an emergency committee meeting at break time."

SIX

Kitan

It's a really nice picture. Iyanu had somehow made me look ethereal standing in the firelight.

Truly beautiful.

And that's what magnifies the conflicting emotions. The dichotomy of something I love so much, coupled with words so achingly hurtful. And the switch that flicks between each one is just flipping the Polaroid over.

Oliver is only going to the ball with you because of a bet.

The words are like a broken record; a motif from an unending composition that echoes the laughter and jeering that have followed me all morning.

When I first came to Wodebury, I had nightmares for weeks about all the ways I wasn't fitting in. Unending images of people making fun of things I didn't know or wouldn't be able to change. Iyanu, having lived here since she was five, helped me for the first two years. And after that, Heather provided a safety buffer. Because even as I figured out the codeswitching, that "tea" sometimes meant your evening meal, and everything in between, it was clear that I still wasn't "accepted." Not until Heather.

And yet, none of the nightmares could have prepared me for today.

It's my own fault really. Oliver always seemed too good to be true. But I'd ignored what my years here at Wodebury—what the world itself—has shown me about love stories for people like me.

Tucking the Polaroid into the inside pocket of my wool blazer, I quickly double-check my hair and makeup in the bathroom mirror before heading out of my dorm block. Heather's called an emergency committee meeting, and she hates when people are late.

And I need her now more than ever.

The Lady Chalford corridors always smell like the lavender-scented polish used to clean the old wood flooring, and they creak softly under my feet with every fourth step I take. I tap lightly on my violin case, keeping pace with the sound, and the gentle rhythm helps calm my mind as I prepare to see, and be seen, by people again. It also helps steer my thoughts away from the words on the Polaroid.

But when I step out into the wide-open courtyard, Oliver is leaning against the redbrick wall of the building, tapping his fingers rapidly against his violin case.

My heart clenches.

I'd managed to avoid him and all his texts the entire morning. Clearly, he's changed tactics.

I must make a sound because he glances up and then stumbles upright. "Kitan," he says, running a hand through his floppy hair. "Hey, I—"

I don't wait for him to continue, turning swiftly and speeding away.

"No, wait!"

I don't slow down, heart pounding harder as I exit to the lakeside. The banks are covered in mallards making their way to the lawns by Brookfield, and I hurriedly rush past them to start across the bridge.

"Please!"

Maybe I'm tired from the sudden sprint, or maybe it's the strangled note in his voice, like a misplaced violin strum. Whichever one, it stops me in place halfway across the bridge.

Oliver takes a deep breath, and I can practically feel the air behind me shift as he moves to stand in front of me, arm gently brushing mine. I shiver, keeping my eyes locked on the violin case clutched tightly in his left hand.

"Kitan, I'm so sorry." His voice sounds heavy with sincerity. "It's all just a misunderstanding."

The words on the Polaroid seemed quite clear to me.

"I can explain everything."

I finally meet his gaze, and whatever he sees in mine stops him from saying more. I recognize the pain in his expression, but it can't be as bad as the feelings twisting inside me.

"Did you ever really want to go with me?"

"Yes! The bet was just . . . You see, all the rugby guys were there watching, and I couldn't say no."

A group of lower schoolers come through the arch from the main courtyard behind him, catching my attention. "Keep your voice down," I urge softly. Desperately. "Please."

Oliver's words halt on his lips again, and there's a long silence as we wait for the group to walk past. Even through my own hazy vision, I can see the wet sheen over his eyes, which stay locked on mine for the short moment it takes the lower schoolers to move out of hearing distance. It feels like an hour.

Biting my lip, I brush the hot wetness from my cheeks, and finally look away. The sky is so gray; it'll probably start raining soon.

"Did you get one too?" My words are almost silent, and he responds in kind.

"Yeah."

"What did it say?"

Oliver shuffles on his feet. "Nonsense about how dating you won't make me popular. I threw it away after."

And that hurts. Because it's true. It's why the few guys who'd briefly

63

considered me at the matchmaking event all hesitated and ultimately decided I wasn't worth it.

But Oliver was supposed to be different.

The sound of thunder rumbles above us.

"So, going with me was just a game to you?"

"No, I wanted to. I—I promise."

I can't ignore the way his voice cracks, and I sway closer to him for a brief second before catching myself and standing firm.

"I don't think I want to talk to you anymore." The words push past the ache in my throat. "It's a good thing the Bach piece finally works, so we don't need to practice anymore."

"Kitan."

"And please don't text me again."

I pull out my umbrella as the first raindrops begin to fall, then make my way around him.

"Please, Kitan, let's talk about this."

A hiccuping sob escapes my lips as I glance back over my shoulder.

"I have to get to this meeting; I can't be late. Heather hates when people are late for stuff."

The rain is falling faster now, pattering hard on the umbrella above my head, and as I watch it soak his hair, slide down the bridge of his nose and over his lips, I want to share it with him.

I squeeze tight on the handle. "This could have been really great," I say, gesturing tiredly between us.

He takes a breath in. "It still can be."

"Can it?"

The silence that follows as he tries to find the words is enough.

I turn away, and head quickly to the library.

SEVEN

Iyanu

It's raining heavily now.

The sunlight filtering in through the clouds earlier have now lost their battle, and so an eerie glow blankets my path from art class to the impromptu committee meeting.

I have no real way to prove my innocence. And even if I did, the deed is already done. In the space of a weekend, my world turned upside down, and in the unlikely event that Mr. Leighton hasn't heard about this yet, it won't be long until he does. Not to mention, Heather and Quincy aren't going to the ball together anymore, which would mean nothing to me if I wasn't at the center of it.

What was it that Navin had said?

A hellscape.

This will probably be the end of my place on the committee.

Last week, that idea might have been welcome, but now it just leaves a bitter taste in my mouth.

After Navin and I parted ways from the darkroom to go to class, I made a pit stop at the art wing bathrooms to unpack my hair and fluff it out into an afro. The thick cloud of tight coils was supposed to act as a barrier between my periphery and all the watching eyes. But now, as I head toward the main library, it doesn't matter. I can still hear the whispers, and I desperately yearn for my phone so I can stuff in my earphones and blast my favorite playlist.

I hurry across the atrium toward the library, and when I finally get there, Navin is waiting for me outside the large doors. "Everyone's already down in the private study room."

I tug on the strap of my camera, returned to its rightful place around my neck, and the gentle weight is comforting against my chest.

"All right, let's go."

The library is mostly empty, the usual break time crowd probably out dealing with the fallout of the Polaroids. There are only a few students dotted around the long mahogany tables, stacks of leather-bound books sitting next to their laptops as they type away. The same eerie glow fills the grand space, the Gothic arched windows on the balcony level sending light down through the banisters that cast long shadows on the tall bookcases below.

We make our way through the dusty stacks to the winding stone staircase at the back of the library, and the shuffle of our feet joins the echo of the rain in the dark stairwell.

When we get to the bottom, I grab Navin's arm.

The study room is just ahead, the soft murmurings of conversation indecipherable behind the heavy wooden door.

"It'll be okay, babe. I've got you." Navin pulls the door open.

Awkward would be too kind a description as all conversations cease, leaving only a deafening silence.

Everyone is here. All seven of the other committee members. But it's like they're not here at all. Not the usual them anyway. There's a simmering anger hanging in the air, one that isn't solely directed at me.

Heather, Sarah, and Kitan are sitting together as always, but Sarah's at the head of the table, the position typically reserved for Heather. Sarah fidgets a little, and she keeps sneaking glances at Kitan, whose eyes are trained firmly on the table in front of her.

The starkest change though is with Luc and the twins. Their trio is completely split up. Luc's usual laid-back attitude is nowhere to be found; instead he sits brooding on the large windowsill at the back of the room, detached from the whole group and glaring angrily out at the rain. Jordan is slumped low in his chair, reading something on his phone. He's sitting on Quincy's left, way across the table from Marcus, whose arm is draped around Heather's shoulders.

Quincy stares at the pair like someone's kicked his puppy, and I turn back to Marcus and Heather again, before glancing over at Sarah.

My insides thrum with discomfort.

Quincy had said that Heather ended things with them for the ball, but Sarah and Marcus are supposed to be official now, right?

I turn to Navin, the question in my eyes, but he looks just as confused as I feel.

Heather, however, looks like her usual self: smug face, done up in the wrong shade of foundation, pinched with ire as she shifts her glare from me to Quincy, and then back again.

Gathering myself, I hold my head up as Navin and I weave around the tables toward the free seats at the back of the room. I try to catch Kitan's eye as we walk past her, but she just stares determinedly down at the table.

I slump low in my chair, desperate to keep my heart steady. After another beat, Sarah finally breaks the silence.

"So, I got a call from the events guy at Dalworth Golf Club, and he wants someone to come down this week to finalize location stuff for the ball."

She pauses, and it's obvious she wants someone to volunteer, but we all just stare at each other silently.

Then Navin shifts in his seat. "We'll go," he says, pointing to me as though it's not obvious who he meant.

"Okay—" But Sarah is interrupted.

"We'll go too," Quincy says, nudging Jordan.

Without looking up from his phone, the younger brother sighs. "Yeah, sure."

Heather scoffs, flicking her hair over her shoulder, and I grit my teeth.

"Shall I tell the events guy Wednesday?" Sarah asks.

"We've got Career Day on Wednesday." Kitan's eyes widen with surprise, like she didn't mean to speak, and she quickly drops her gaze back to the table.

"Yeah, I suppose that might be a bit too much for one day," Sarah agrees, mumbling to herself as she looks through her brown leather planner.

I try once again to meet Kitan's gaze; she doesn't make eye contact, focusing on the apparently fascinating patterns on the table.

Uncertainty slowly creeps up my spine.

What was written on her Polaroid?

Sarah seems to find whatever she was looking for in her planner because she smiles. "Right, how about Thursday?"

The four of us glance at each other, checking for consensus, but I have to turn swiftly away from Quincy's imploring gaze.

"Sure," Navin confirms.

"Brilliant," Sarah says, then she turns to me. "It's good you're going. He has two location options for the indoor photography and he needs someone to choose between them before they can set up the decor."

I don't get to respond because Heather scoffs again. This time though, she finally speaks. "So, what? We're really just going to ignore the elephant in the room?"

And there it is.

Navin takes my hand under the table, squeezing tight. But it's funny. Now that the confrontation is here, my bubbling anger from Heather's scoffs dissolves my fear.

I didn't do this. I'm not going to sit here afraid like I have something to hide.

No one says anything for a few seconds, and then Luc speaks, smirking. "I don't know, Heather, whatever do you mean?"

"Chill out, man," Marcus responds, and Heather smiles at him before turning to me with a glare.

"You want to tell us why you spread all those lies about everyone?"

At this Marcus glances at Sarah, shaking his head in disappointment before looking away.

Luc snorts. "Are you really one to be talking about lies right now, Heather?"

She scoffs again, but surprisingly it's Jordan who responds. "Are *you* really the one to be pointing any fingers?"

Luc throws him a harsh glare, and Sarah quickly pipes up. "How about we all calm down."

Marcus chuckles mirthlessly. "Wow. She says we should calm down."

The words come at the same time as Luc curses under his breath in French. He turns to Sarah with a sneer and says, "Pretty sure no one was talking to you."

Sarah's eyes darken, but Jordan interrupts whatever she was going to say. "*Really* nice, bro."

Luc rolls his eyes. "Whatever, *bro*."

A deep thrill of curiosity ignites within me at the entire exchange, a heady rush that's completely unexpected. Just for a moment, I feel something other than contempt for the Polaroids.

What was written on theirs?

I glance over at Kitan again but she's still avoiding my eyes, sitting motionless like she's trying to disappear.

Then Quincy sighs. "Come on, Heather, you really think Iyanu did this?"

My eyes snap to his.

It's hard to decipher his expression, some mix between hope and embarrassment.

I look away.

"Well, *she* took the photos at the matchmaking event, and *she* didn't get a Polaroid," Heather snaps back. "Obviously, it was her."

Navin squeezes my hand again, and I grit my teeth harder.

"I didn't do it," I bite out. "Why would I?"

Luc responds this time. "Well, you're always behind that camera. Skulking around. I wouldn't be surprised if you go around listening to everyone's conversations too. Mrs. Tarar says it all the time in photography class: 'Know your subjects.'"

I roll my eyes so hard it's a wonder they don't fall out my head. Luc is the only one on the committee I share more than one class with; unfortunately, we all have English Literature together.

"That doesn't check out at all," Navin says. "Iyanu's not the one in this room with a history of spreading rumors." There's a tense pause as everyone but Heather averts their eyes. "And whoever did it stole her binder with really important negatives that she needs to get back."

"Oh, boo hoo. I'm pretty sure that—" Heather's angry words are cut off by Sarah's planner falling to the floor.

"Oops," she says as we all turn to her in unison. Her eyes flash to mine briefly, and I can almost tell that she dropped the planner on purpose to cut the tension. "I just don't know. If Iyanu did it, surely she'd send a Polaroid to herself. To cover her tracks?"

"Exactly," Quincy says.

Ignoring him, I send Sarah a grateful smile and she returns it tentatively. But Heather's eyes narrow at her, and something potent passes between them.

After a few tense seconds, Heather seems to decide to let it go, turning back to me.

"Either way, I've spoken to Mr. Leighton, and he has most of the Polaroids now so that's proof enough. You'll be off the committee soon. Maybe even expelled."

I try my best not to freak out, but it's hard when the back of my eyes start prickling.

Maybe it's some kind of latent reaction I haven't lost from the days when it was us against the world, but I turn to Quincy instinctively. His brows crease in concern and he immediately claps his hands together to get everyone's attention. "Okay, let's just get back to the meeting."

A scuffling sound, followed by a tentative knock at the door sends all our heads swinging around.

Quincy sighs. "Come in."

In walks a tiny Year Seven, his long tie done up so tightly it's a wonder he can breathe, much less speak. His eyes fall on me.

"Iyanu?"

I nod slowly.

"Mr. Leighton wants to see you in his office."

Mr. Leighton must have taken his prize-winning mare out this morning because his usual tailored suit is replaced by jodhpurs and a polo, his gray eyes bright with contentment.

I settle down hesitantly in the leather wingback in front of the vintage partners desk, and Mr. Leighton takes his place behind it.

"So, Iyanu. Quite the stir we have here, isn't it?"

Ever since I started at Wodebury, Mr. Leighton has always made his best effort to pronounce my name correctly. And he pretty much always gets it right. But every time he says it, his conservative RP accent makes the vowels sound like some sort of grand declaration: "EE-yAH-noo." So like always, despite my nerves, I have to hold back a giggle at his almost cartoonish poshness.

He was a Wodebrian decades ago, before he came back to teach here and was named head of Year Twelve.

"I guess so, Sir."

He smiles, leaning forward to open one of the desk drawers. "Indeed."

As he rifles for whatever he's looking for, I try to calm myself by scanning the titles of the volumes in the bookcases behind him.

It's clear that Mr. Leighton fancies himself a bit of a "worldly Renaissance man." The shelves are lined with tomes on philosophy and science in all manner of languages, and each one is leather bound. Landscape oil paintings hang on the pale walls, and dotted around the office are white stone sculptures and Greek stand displays of ancient plates and artifacts.

A soft thud draws my attention back to Mr. Leighton.

On the desk is a stack of the infamous Polaroids. There's no doubt that these are my photos from the matchmaking event—the ones I'd hung up to dry in the darkroom now shrunk down to . . . this.

In this form, these photos simultaneously mean nothing and everything to me.

I look back up at Mr. Leighton.

He motions for me to take them, the weathered crow's feet etched into his white skin deepening as he frowns. But it feels more like concern than anger. Like he's trying to read my face.

As I reach forward, I take a breath to try to settle my nerves.

Considering the havoc they'd wreaked, the Polaroids aren't as heavy as I'd expected. I trail my fingers over the sharp corners before shuffling through them, slowly turning each one over to read the messages.

The words boast all manner of ridiculous claims, but they're just sensible enough to make the reader stop. They're words that could be true if you think hard enough. Words that can crumble the foundation of your relationships if there was already a crack.

I lean back a little in the chair, angling the Polaroids toward the light.

Now that I have more of a handle on my emotions, I notice things I missed when I saw the first three. Whoever did this had the foresight not to write the messages by hand so they could avoid identification. The inky words were clearly written on the back by a computer, the letters too perfectly spaced and angled the same in each message.

I'm about to shuffle to the next one when Mr. Leighton coughs. I look up again, startled at how easily they were able to draw me in.

"I've been doing a bit of sleuthing this morning, gathering up as much evidence as I could." He pauses, gesturing to the stack in my hands. "I wasn't able to get them all, but it seems whoever did this has spun quite the tale. From the other Year Twelve students I've spoken to, most don't want to believe the claims are true, but the damage has already been done."

"Okay." I'm not sure what else to say.

Mr. Leighton watches me carefully. "They all seem to think you did this."

I clutch tightly at my camera strap and his eyes follow the motion.

"And what do you think, Sir?" I ask, cautiously.

His eyes meet mine again. "Well, they are your photos, aren't they?" My chest tightens. "So, what I'm trying to figure out is who has it out for you."

That gives me pause.

I study his eyes for a long moment, trying to figure out what he's thinking. It doesn't feel like a trap, but you never know.

He continues. "Because I certainly can't see you having done this. You, and your cousin, are one of the good ones."

We sit in silence for a few moments, neither of us saying anything as Mr. Leighton seems to realize what he's said.

One of the good ones.

Phrases like this are par for the course here at Wodebury, but under the circumstances, I can't even bring myself to be rightfully angry about it. I just hold his gaze, blinking.

Shifting uncomfortably, Mr. Leighton clears his throat. "Yes. So, any thoughts?"

I look down at the stack again, shuffling to the next Polaroid.

"Sir, I really don't have—"

It's Luc's Polaroid. He's standing there on the stage, the blurred motion of his hands perfectly capturing his exuberance as the matchmaking event host.

I turn the Polaroid over.

Heather used Luc.
Then dumped him because he's not even second best.

Frowning, I read it again.

Heather has dated a few of the rugby guys—Luc first, and now it seems Marcus too. But Luc and Heather broke up way back in Year Nine, their short relationship started when she'd first arrived at Wodebury and ended just as quickly.

My heart speeds up as I shuffle to the next one, ignoring Mr. Leighton clearing his throat again.

The shot is taken through the trees. Sarah sits there laughing by the bonfire, looking almost pixie-like in her flowy green blouse.

I know you cheated on Marcus.

It makes no sense. Sarah and Marcus started getting closer around the end of last term, but they only officially got together when they were paired at the matchmaking event on Friday.

Why would whoever did this lie on some Polaroids, but tell the truth on others? Or are all the messages just designed to cause the maximum amount of chaos?

I think about the Polaroids I got from Navin and Quincy and compare the wording of all the messages. Some speak directly to the recipient while others just talk about the people involved.

Could this have been done by more than one person?

74

Mr. Leighton clears his throat once more, trying to get my attention, but I move to the next one.

Marcus. He's sitting in the foreground with Jordan blurred beside him, the light from the bonfire hitting his face just right.

You don't have what it takes and everyone knows it.

I quickly shuffle through to the last Polaroid, not even bothering to read the messages on the others.

"Iyanu, I've decided that we're going to have a Year Twelve assembly tomorrow afternoon to get to the bottom of this."

Those words send my gaze flying back to Mr. Leighton.

"But I need to know," he continues, "do you have any idea who could have done this?"

I shake my head. "No idea, Sir."

With only Kitan's and Jordan's Polaroids missing, I've now seen most of the other committee members' Polaroids. Each message I've seen is just as confusing as the last—yet damaging enough to create the mess I'd witnessed at the meeting.

Mr. Leighton carries on speaking, but his earlier declaration suddenly shakes loose a thought.

Does someone have it out for the popular crowd?

Something else sparks in my mind as I remember what Navin said in the darkroom earlier.

"Only the people at the top would know these kinds of secrets."

Plus, only the other committee members knew that I'd be working in the darkroom through the weekend. They're the only ones who knew where my matchmaking event photos would be.

Was it one of them who did this?

Glancing back down at the Polaroids, I think about the meeting—the hidden conversations behind the words thrown back and forth. If these messages are true, it's not like just anyone could know these intimate things about the group that practically runs our year. It has to be someone on the inside. Right?

There's only one way to find out for sure.

Even as the thought lands, I realize I've already decided to investigate.

I don't care about the Polaroids. Sure, whoever released them stole my photos in order to put the blame on me for whatever twisted vendetta they have. But they also stole the negatives from the Black Girls Winter Fair. And I *have* to get them back. I can't write the *WeCreate* photo article without them. I need that job.

I meet Mr. Leighton's eyes once again.

"Can I borrow these, Sir?" His brows crease slightly, so before he can object, I quickly plow on. "Whoever did this stole my negatives too, Sir. I can't print these again. All my photos are gone." His expression softens a little, so I carry on. "Please, I just need to scan them and blow them up to full size. I'll bring the Polaroids right back."

My throat clenches with the reality of the situation. If I can't have copies of these, I have to hope I have all their messages memorized.

There's a brief silence as Mr. Leighton considers, and I do my best to look as desperate as possible. Because I am.

Maybe he still feels a little guilty about the "good ones" comment, because a few moments later, he sighs. "Fine. But keep them to yourself; they can't go spreading around again. I want them right back on my desk before lunchtime."

I'm already nodding before he even finishes. He doesn't seem to think all this was me, but *this* is a test if I ever saw one. He's trying to definitively rule me out as a suspect.

"I'll bring them right back, Sir."

"I'm serious. If they end up going around again, I'll know it was you who had them last. Whatever happens then will be up to the headmaster."

I nod quickly, straightening out the stack and using the hairband around my wrist to secure them together with Luc's Polaroid at the top of the pile.

"Thank you, Sir," I say, rising to my feet. It comes out a little distracted, my mind already too focused on the task at hand.

I'll have to watch all the committee members carefully and do my own digging to figure out which one of them could have done this. Exactly what they accused me of.

I almost chuckle at the irony.

EIGHT

Iyanu

One minute I'm alone, putting my stuff into the back of my car after classes; the next, Quincy is standing right beside me.

A loud yelp escapes my lips, and I try to play it off. But judging by his smirk, I fail.

Quincy has been trying to talk to me all afternoon, somehow always turning up in the same wing as me despite having no classes there. I'd admire his perseverance if I wasn't trying to stay under the radar to subtly observe "The Magnificent Seven."

Holding in a heavy sigh, I shut the boot and turn my attention to him.

"What do you want, Quincy?"

He raises an eyebrow, a playful look in his eyes.

"You've been avoiding me."

This time I do sigh, but I hold back my eye roll and that should count for something.

"I've been avoiding everyone."

Quincy's smirk turns into a full-on grin.

"Where are you off to? Home?"

"Yes," I say, brushing past him to the driver side. The rain has reduced to a gentle spittle but judging by the gray clouds still hanging around, it's far from over. "I'm going to grab Feyi from her friend's dorm in Roweton."

"Oh, I'm headed to Roweton! Give me a ride?"

I eye him skeptically.

Out of the fifteen houses at Wodebury Hall, Roweton is the farthest away from the main building. It's a twenty-minute walk (but a five-minute drive) and if you don't live there, one generally avoids going. Navin, whose dorm is in Roweton—the same house his dad, grandad, and on up his family tree had lived in when they were Wodebrians—regularly complains about it.

Quincy, however, is in Brookfield House, and so are the twins. If he'd wanted me to drop him off there or at Lady Chalford right next to it, maybe his request would make sense.

"Oh? How come?" I ask.

It's clear from the way his eyes widen that he didn't expect me to inquire, which is silly, because we don't do this. Not anymore. And yet, here he is, asking for a ride and being super chill like the last three years hadn't happened.

"I . . . Luc! He has a thing. Told me to meet him in his dorm."

The excuse is laughable, but his rambling words make me realize something. A ride all the way to Roweton could be an opportunity to weasel some information out of him about the group.

"Okay, fine."

"Awesome," he says, grinning happily as he opens the passenger door and jumps in. The cheerful innocence softens my heart a little, and I get in too.

As usual, it takes a few tries but eventually my car sputters to life. We're silent as I pull out of the Maudhill House parking lot; I try my best to focus on the road instead of the warm but subtle scent of Quincy's citrusy cologne slowly filling the small space. His tall frame squeezed into my tiny secondhand coupe is pretty comical, and I don't bother to stifle my laugh as he shuffles to find a comfortable position for his feet.

"Hey, it's not my fault that I need more leg room," he says, then chuckles. "Have you even grown since Year Seven?"

"Oi! I'm like five three now," I respond, and that has him laughing.

"Sure."

He grabs the aux cord to plug in his phone, and after a few moments spent scrolling through, the gentle sound of a bolero fills the car.

A thrill of familiarity bubbles up inside me, somehow expecting Quincy's usual antics from when we were younger, where he'd put on a ridiculous deep voice to "serenade" me in Spanish.

But of course, that doesn't happen. Instead, Quincy turns the volume down low, and out of my periphery I see that his expression has sobered.

My nerves creep back in.

"So, the Polaroids," Quincy says.

I clench and unclench my hands around the steering wheel.

"I didn't do it."

Quincy startles, the seatbelt grazing his neck as he twists hurriedly in his seat to face me. "No! I know. I just was gonna say . . ." He glances out the windscreen. "I was gonna say, we should try and figure out who did do it together."

I barely contain my snort of surprise.

We're halfway to Roweton now, the large Georgian building standing at the end of the long road down the hill. But I have to refrain from speeding up to get there faster and end this conversation, weaseling information out of Quincy be damned.

"What do you mean 'together'?" I ask, glad that my voice remains steady.

He faces forward again. "Everything with Heather and Marcus . . . well, you know. And now Jordan is icing him out and Luc as well. Although, Luc's not really talking to any of us anyway, and I just know there's something more Jordan isn't saying, but nothing makes sense anymore."

That messy swirl of information confirms what I'd already deduced at the meeting, but I can tell there's so much more he's leaving out.

"What happened?" I ask, hoping my calm tone covers my probing.

Quincy runs a hand over his plaits, as he seemingly makes a decision. "Did you know that Marcus had a panic attack this morning in form?"

I frown. When we were younger, Marcus would have really bad intrusive thoughts. They'd come seemingly out of nowhere, and then suddenly he'd be hyperventilating from a panic attack.

I didn't realize they were still happening.

"No, I didn't," I whisper.

Quincy nods. "The twins have been arguing because he's had more panic attacks recently. Jordan wants him to slow down on this rugby stuff. Mr. Forrester has been trying to do the same too; he's considering keeping him at the Premiership level instead of putting him forward to try out for the England under-17s academy. All that pressure." Quincy releases a heavy sigh. "But this morning, Jordan just pretended not to care. I think he's tired of pleading to a brick wall. He stormed out of form after Marcus ran out. Well, as best as Jordan can storm out with a fractured ankle."

Quincy mutters about getting Jordan to the hospital to adjust his crutches, and I warm with the familiarity of the simultaneous frustration and care that comes with having siblings.

"Was it because of the Polaroids? This morning's panic attack?"

"Yeah," he says, expression grim. "I need to find out who did this."

We sit in silence as we descend the hill, the Roweton building cresting before us, and I consider this new information. This pretty much rules out Quincy. It's possible that it could have been him and these were unintended consequences, but it just can't be. He'd never do that to his brothers.

The twins came exactly eleven months after Quincy did, about three weeks before his first birthday. Tío Félix always used to joke about the twins' antics, saying that Quincy should have warned them that there was trouble to come when he was born.

There's barely an age gap between them, but Quincy is definitely the older brother. He's always protecting them, no matter what.

I certainly know that life.

The thought softens my heart a little bit more. That was part of the reason Quincy and I had bonded so fast and so fully when we'd first met.

As I pull into a space in the Roweton parking lot, the silence continues, stretching on as we sit there with the gentle bolero floating through the speakers.

I try to think of something to say, but Quincy shifts in his seat again, eyes meeting mine.

"So? You wanna try and figure this out together?"

It's the exact opposite of what I'd decided to do just hours ago. If I work with Quincy, who knows how quickly the rest of the group will find out I'm investigating. He might not even think it's one of them. Getting back those negatives from the fair is just too important to risk this all blowing up, and not for the first time today, I feel the weight of the *WeCreate* deadline pushing down on my shoulders.

"The person who did this stole all my negatives, Quincy, including ones that I need for this job I'm trying to get. It's really important. I have to get them back."

He must see the worry in my eyes because he doesn't say anything, just nods with a sober expression.

I sigh. "I'll think about it."

Feyi hurries into the house seconds after I park the car, her bag of electronics jangling at her side, desperate to get started on . . . Well, she'd spent the entire ride explaining it, uncharacteristically worried about the coding project she'd been putting together for the past week, but I couldn't really follow the intricacies.

The rain has started back up again, so I quickly grab my stuff from the boot and sprint inside. I chuckle as I turn on the hallway light. Feyi didn't even bother to do so in her hurry to get to the kitchen and start work on her project.

I shove off my Docs, placing them next to her Kickers on the rack by the door, before making my way up the hallway. There's a gentle melody coming from the living room, the only other light on besides the one from the kitchen at the end of the hall. After the sheer turbulence of the day, my heart brightens as I realize what's going on. Dropping my things at the bottom of the stairs, I head over to peek through the slightly ajar door.

As expected, Dad has brought the record player down from my room, and he and Mum are slow dancing to the smooth jazzy song. Her head is tucked gently under his chin, their dark brown skin like gold in the dim light of the side table lamp.

I lean quietly against the doorframe, wrapping my arms around my middle.

They always try to do this whenever they spend more than sixteen hours away from each other—a way to reconnect and get back in sync, especially after Mum's had a hectic shift at the hospital. It's a pact Mum said they'd made after they got married. And they pretty much always stick to it.

Mum's eyes are closed, but I can tell she's a little weary. She's out of her nurse's scrubs, her soft ankara dress clenched in the palm of Dad's hand where it rests on her waist, arms wrapped safely around her.

I sigh.

It's hard to imagine being that in love.

Turning back into the hallway, I follow the scent of coconut rice and èfó to the kitchen, stomach rumbling. After scanning the Polaroids and getting them back to Mr. Leighton before the lunch bell, I'd only been able to scarf down a cereal bar as I hid in the photography lab.

Feyi is sitting at the table, already working on the coding project, and from where I'm standing it might as well be the pilot's console of a warp-capable starship. She's wearing a deep frown, something a little more than her usual concentration, and her shoulders are wound up tensely.

Before I can ask about it, she looks up. "I forgot to say in the car. I texted you but you didn't respond—"

My gasp cuts her off. *My phone!*

All thoughts of food disappear, and I jerk around to sprint up to my room, but I'm stopped by the presence of Mum and Dad standing in the doorway.

"My phone," I say, trying to hurry past, but Dad chuckles and gently holds my shoulders to stop me.

"Pleaseeee, I have to get it," I whine, not caring enough to be embarrassed at my childish tone.

Mum laughs. "Calm down," she says, heading toward the pot of rice on the cooker. "Do you want some? We have to talk to you about something."

The way she says it, like she's trying deliberately to sound nonchalant, sends alarm bells ringing in my mind.

I turn back to Feyi, the question heavy in my eyes. At least the little sneak feels bad enough to look sheepish.

"That's what I was texting you about. I told them what happened."

I *just* hold in my growl.

"Don't be upset with her," Dad says, steering Mum to sit down, and moving to fix me a plate of food instead. He's still wearing his long paint-splattered jeans, so he probably spent the whole afternoon in the dining room turned studio finishing off his new piece. "I'm glad we know. Maybe we can help?"

Deflating, I lean back against the doorframe.

Mum's got a gentle smile on, and the expression warms me. They can try, but I have no idea how they can help with this.

"It's okay. I'm sorting it out. I spoke to Mr. Leighton and there's gonna be an assembly tomorrow."

Dad places my full plate on the table then settles down next to Mum, tying his locs back with the hairband around his wrist. My stomach growls again, but my need for my phone is stronger.

"What about your photos?" Mum asks. "For the *WeCreate* article?"

My stomach clenches.

"Whoever did it took them," I grit out. Mum and Dad exchange a look, but I carry on before they can say anything. "It's fine. I just need to go get my phone."

I move to leave but pause midmotion, turning back to grab the plate of food—because *food*—before hurrying out the kitchen. "Thank you!"

Hopping carefully over my things on the bottom step, I take the stairs two at a time and burst into my room. My phone is sitting on my dressing table now, and I dash over to grab it, placing my food to the side as I settle down on the chair.

The notifications flood in as I turn off the "do not disturb" from last night. Tons of texts from Navin, Mum, Dad, and Feyi.

I stand there reading through them all as the rain comes back full and strong, slamming hard against the window; it's difficult to believe that it was this morning that my shoe was hiding on the windowsill.

The burn of tears starts up behind my eyes again.

I was standing here just hours ago doing Feyi's hair, expecting to be back here with the photos, laptop in tow and ready to write the *WeCreate* article.

My phone buzzes, and I wipe away the tears that've escaped.

A text from Quincy.

Monday 4:07 P.M.

Q

hey yaya, this is still your number, right?

The nickname makes the tears fall a little harder.

> yeah, it is

It only takes a few seconds for him to respond.

> you know who it is?

I chuckle wetly, wiping at my snotty nose.

> yeah. "yaya" gave it away.

I hesitate briefly before sending the next text.

> plus, I still have your number saved. never deleted it.

The response comes in instantly.

> me either.

NINE

Kitan

I'm hit by a wall of sound the moment I pull open the door of the Lady Chalford dining hall. The room is filled to the brim, only a handful of empty seats left at the three walnut dining tables that run the length of the space. Loud conversations and the sound of chairs scraping against the stone floor echo off the vaulted ceilings. It's definitely not just the lower schoolers, who actually have to come to breakfast every morning, but practically every Lady Chalford Sixth Former is in here too.

Dinner yesterday was the same; everybody getting together to discuss the messages written on the Polaroids—and there's no doubt that they all know what was written on mine.

At least I know what's on theirs too.

Unsurprisingly, the thought doesn't make me feel better, especially when I notice a group of Year Ten students giggling when they spot me.

Looking around the room, I see Heather, Sarah, Marcus, and a few of the other rugby players sitting at the end of the table on the right, next to the house parents' dais. Even from here, I can see that they've almost finished their meals.

I sigh.

The nightmares have come back. Images of laughing faces, pointing fingers, whispered voices repeating the words from my Polaroid. After tossing and turning for hours, I'd finally fallen asleep around four and ended up sleeping through my alarm.

And now I'm late.

I quickly head to the cloister leading into the food station, grabbing a tray from the racks and joining the queue. As we slowly make our way through the arches, the conversations from the hall are replaced with the dinner ladies' morning banter, and the delicious scent of food grows stronger.

Then someone taps my shoulder.

"Hey, Kitan, is it true?"

I don't recognize the white girl in line behind me, but I smile anyway. Even as she shifts closer into my personal space.

"Is what true?"

"You and Oliver are over?"

Her initial overfamiliarity was uncomfortable, but these words make it worse.

Nothing would make me happier than to snap at her to mind her own business, but I can't.

"Yes. It's true."

The girl either doesn't notice my discomfort, or doesn't care, because she just nods and continues. "I was actually so surprised you guys were even going together in the first place."

Whatever she was going to say next dies in her throat as she catches sight of the flare of anger that briefly shows through my carefully neutral facade.

She changes tack.

"Iyanu's your cousin, right? I wonder how she knew that Jordan's been lying about being gay this entire time?"

I frown. "Wait. What do you mean?"

"You know? With Jordan's Polaroid. It said that he's just been faking being gay to be like 'special' or whatever so he stands out from Marcus. And it totally makes sense now. Because why else would he not have dated anyone yet? He's been out for like a whole year. So yeah, anyway, how did Iyanu find out?"

Her words come out in a quick rush, and I stare at her for a long moment.

What she's saying doesn't even make sense—that's not how this works. Iyanu and I have never dated anyone, but I still know I'm straight and she still knows she's bi. It has nothing to do with how you act or who you're with.

Do people actually think that's what Jordan's Polaroid is about? Because it's obviously not true.

So that means some of the Polaroids are lies.

Sarah's and now Jordan's too.

A small voice in my head thinks about Oliver, wishes that the message on mine wasn't true either. But there's no point in that, so I push the thought away.

I put on an overly confused expression. "I don't understand what you mean by that. Please explain it to me."

The girl starts to speak but suddenly stops herself, pale cheeks flushing.

"I mean, it's, uhh, just what I've heard," she sputters, but then quickly collects herself. "Haven't you heard what everyone's saying?" The girl looks surprised, like she truly expected me to be on top of all this, and I realize that I've dropped the ball.

After the meeting yesterday, I spent every moment that I wasn't in classes in my room, keeping my head down. But I can't afford to do that; knowing things is how I make the right choices and insulate myself with Heather and the others. It's how I ultimately survive this place—it's the only thing that works.

I've been so focused on Oliver and my own Polaroid, that I haven't been keeping a close enough eye on the fallout of the others'.

Embarrassment rushes through me, but I don't let it show.

"Well," I start, willing the line to hurry up. "I don't know anything about that, but it can't be true. Besides, I'm not Iyanu's keeper." I chuckle, hoping it doesn't sound forced, and luckily the girl returns the laughter.

Mercifully, we get to the front of the queue before the girl can respond, and I move through my order as quickly as possible without making it obvious. Two hard eggs? Yes, thank you. Baked beans? Sounds lovely, thank you. Crumpets? Perfect, thank you.

When I exit the cloister at the other end of the hall, I'm startled at the sight of Marcus standing at the drinks table.

He throws me a look, tilting his head, and I glance over at the others before quickly joining him.

"Act natural," he whispers.

I snort. Even without the loud rumble of conversations, we're far enough away from the others for the hushed tone to be unnecessary, but I follow suit.

"What's wrong?" I busy myself with slowly filling a glass of water just like he is.

"She's not happy."

I don't have to ask who "she" is, and my mirth immediately recedes. "She'll get over it."

Marcus sighs. "Either way, we're going to have to play this carefully the next few days. She's determined to get everything back in order."

He's right. Because if she's not satisfied, then "order" might mean our—no, *my*—removal.

And maybe I'm too exhausted, but I feel a rush of resentment. It's so surprising that I hesitate a moment too long to file it away, but the sudden feeling of water dripping down my hand snaps me out of it. I quickly put down the jug, blinking away the wetness that started to swell behind my eyes.

Breathe.

I take a long sip to temper the overflow, sifting through and sorting all my emotions back to their respective compartments.

"You okay?" Marcus asks, brows creased in concern.

I nod. "Let's go."

Putting the half-empty glass on my tray, I take a final calming breath before heading over to the others.

"Took you long enough," Heather says, placing her cutlery neatly in the center of her empty plate.

Marcus sits in the space next to her, eyes flicking to Sarah so quickly I almost miss it.

I glance over at her, but she keeps her gaze resolutely away from the twin, before turning back to Heather. "Sorry, I couldn't sleep properly last night, so I woke up later than usual."

"It's fine."

From her expression it's clearly not fine, and my shoulders tense as I take off my coat and settle down in the space Sarah saved for me.

I've barely finished taking my first bite when one of the guys speaks up. "We've just been talking about Iyanu."

I take another bite before I respond. "Cool."

"So? Did you talk to her?"

They're all watching me, but I keep my eyes focused on cutting up my eggs. One of them isn't as hard as the other, part of the yolk is still a little runny, and I section that away to the side of my plate.

"Why would I do that?"

Heather scoffs but doesn't say anything.

"Because I asked you to. Yesterday," the guy whines.

I vaguely recall one of the rugby players approaching me in history class yesterday, but I'd been distracted by the fact that Oliver was sitting just two rows behind me.

"She's ruined everything with my date."

I tilt my head, trying to remember what the guy's Polaroid had said.

Something about him cheating? I cross-reference it with the information I have filed away in my mind on "Recent drama with the rugby players."

"But wasn't that all you? You said things weren't working, and she asked someone else. All that happened *before* the Polaroids came out."

There's a long pause, and I freeze mid-swallow as I realize what I've just said.

I don't say things like that out loud. Certainly not in the middle of breakfast with everyone listening.

Sarah squeezes my thigh, mirroring the feeling inside me, and I carry on eating, hoping the moment will pass.

But Heather breaks the silence. "You're being really feisty today."

My fork scrapes loudly against the bottom of my plate as I freeze again.

Taking a careful breath, I glance at Marcus, but he quickly looks away. *Right.*

Setting down my cutlery, I meet Heather's gaze. Her green eyes appear darker in her overly bronzed face despite the morning light flooding in from the high, arched windows. "I guess I'm just tired." I turn to the guy. "Sorry."

"It's cool. Don't worry about it," he responds.

Heather watches me for a moment and then grins wide. "I really like your dress today."

And somehow the tightness inside me releases instantly. "Thanks."

Like every other day, I'd laid out my outfit the night before. A long rose-colored sheath dress with ruffle sleeves, something I knew Heather would love.

She nods, then turns to Sarah with a smirk.

"It would have looked even nicer with our pearls though. You know, if *somebody* hadn't misplaced hers."

Sarah rolls her eyes good-naturedly. "I honestly have no clue where it could have gone!"

Heather raises a brow, her little smile telling me that she wants to say something more but decides to keep it to herself.

"Well," she starts, gesturing to Marcus. "We're going to try and get to the library before class, so . . ." They rise to their feet. Marcus clearly eager to leave Sarah's presence. "You coming, Sar?"

He freezes, but it doesn't last long, because Sarah shakes her head quickly.

"I've got a free later, so I'll just go then. I'll wait here while Kitan eats."

"Yeah," I jump in. "We'll see you at the assembly later."

We watch as the pair heads off, Marcus throwing an arm around Heather, and within seconds, the rest of the players disappear to another table.

I stare after them as the worry returns full force.

Before all this, they would have stayed with us even after Heather was gone.

Swallowing down the unsteady feeling, I turn to Sarah, but her eyes are still glued to the couple heading out of the dining hall.

"You doing okay?"

Sarah blinks, hazy eyes shifting to mine. "Huh?"

"That." I nod to the door as it shuts. "Marcus and Heather."

A flurry of emotions cross Sarah's face, and her right hand moves to the Tiffany's heart resting against her collarbone. My hand automatically mirrors the motion, and for a long moment, we both stare at each other's silver pendant before dropping our hands back down. Then Sarah lets out a tiny sigh, slumping in her chair.

"I'm annoyed," she says quietly. "One minute, Quincy and Heather are going together, and me and Marcus are official. Then the Polaroids come out, and next thing I know, I've been dumped and *they're* going together," she huffs, but I can hear the hurt underneath it. "I didn't cheat on Marcus. But he won't talk to me."

I glance down at my rapidly cooling breakfast.

"I know, Sarah. It sucks."

We sit there silently for a minute and then Sarah visibly collects herself, sitting up straight. "It's just as well though. I wouldn't have been able to post photos with Marcus as my date anyways. You know how it is, Aunty Irene would've flipped, and I'm not in the mood to deal with her anti-Blackness. Especially because she's the one getting my dress for the ball. We've been designing it together for months."

Turning her words over in my head, my insides twist with discomfort.

I quickly sift through the heaviness, compartmentalizing it away, and focus instead on my best friend's emotions.

Sarah's clearly trying to convince herself that everything's fine. And anyway, one five-minute passing interaction with Irene Pelham was enough to see how anti-Black she was. Marcus shouldn't have to deal with her white nonsense either.

"Besides, I need to focus on the head girl workshop tomorrow. I can't let all these lies and drama with the Polaroids distract me from the bigger picture." Her freckled nose scrunches in frustration. "When Mr. Leighton called me to his office to talk about the Polaroids, he was like, 'You don't want anything affecting your chances.'"

I grimace, and Sarah raises her hands in agreement.

"Right? What am I supposed to do with that? And with Heather going up for it now too, I can't have a story like me cheating on Golden Boy spreading around on top of everything else . . ."

She groans into her palms, and I place a hand on her back comfortingly.

My meeting with Mr. Leighton hadn't been as turbulent. He'd asked about Iyanu and also if I had a Polaroid, and I said that I knew what it said but I didn't know where it was. I don't know if he believed me or not, but I couldn't bring myself to care. Not with everything else I have to deal with.

Sitting up again, Sarah reaches out to squeeze my hand, concern taking over her features.

"Sorry, I know this all sucks for you too. I'm really sorry about how things turned out with my cousin."

Only because of a bet.

"Yeah, me too."

Tuesday 9:07 A.M.

> Ay. Mister Man.

> why won't you just talk to sarah?

Marcus

texting during class hours? really?

> she didn't cheat. it's as simple as that. i don't know how many times i have to keep saying it.

it isn't that simple. you of all people know that.

> what aren't you saying?

it doesn't matter

listen, i have to go, my teacher is getting suspicious

> fine. but let's meet up after the assembly, we're not done with this conversation.

TEN

Iyanu

The end of class bell trills through the air, but a rush of nerves keeps me from moving.

Things have mostly calmed down today. I'd gotten a few angry glares and comments, but starting the day off with double photography had acted as a balm for what was coming right after.

Mr. Leighton's assembly.

Now whatever respite I've had all morning will be gone once everyone's attention is drawn back to me again. Mr. Leighton probably won't mention my name, but he wouldn't have to. Everyone knows whose photos they are.

". . . and don't be afraid to make mistakes!"

Mrs. Tarar's words to everyone else's retreating backs jolt me out of my thoughts. I quickly scramble to pack up my things and hang my camera around my neck.

"Are you okay?"

I meet Mrs. Tarar's brown eyes, nodding shakily with a tiny smile.

Mrs. Tarar has always been my favorite teacher, not least because she's Pakistani and thus the only woman of color on the Wodebury Hall staff. But a few years ago, she'd pushed for the school to start an A level photography course, which she now teaches as well as her usual English Literature classes.

"I'm all right, Miss."

"Are you sure?" she asks, tucking a strand of her long dark hair behind her ear. "Is it all this business with the Polaroids? I was sorry to hear about your binder."

Her concerned expression is heartwarming, but I really don't want to think about this yet. Not until I get to the assembly and it becomes unavoidable.

I nod more convincingly this time. "Thanks, Miss. But don't worry, it's okay."

She clearly doesn't buy it, but she decides to leave it and her smile brightens. "You're still doing photography for Career Day tomorrow, right?"

I nod, returning the smile.

Every year, the students from the primary school in town, Hanwood, spend the day with Wodebury Hall's Year Twelves for Career Day. We choose one subject from our timetable to teach all day, working with the kids to show them the ropes. And just for fun, everyone, including the kids, gets to dress up as whatever they wanted to be growing up. Everything from an astronaut to Freddie Mercury or Iron Man. I've looked forward to being one of the Year Twelves on Career Day ever since I was a Hanwood student coming to visit Wodebury.

"Brilliant. So after we finish the scheduled tasks with our Hanwood students, Mr. Forrester asked if I could photograph the Year Twelve boys' Career Day rugby match for the school's newsletter. Would you like to join me?"

Another reason Mrs. Tarar is my favorite teacher: she always mentors me and the other BIPOC photography students whenever she can.

I grin. "Definitely. Thank you so much, Miss."

"Of course." Then she waves me on. "All right, don't let me keep you from the assembly."

I wish.

"See you in fifth period."

I head out of the photography lab, grateful that Navin is waiting for me at my locker, but as I start toward him, someone calls my name.

Oliver Wei.

His expression is skittish, eyes darting up and down the corridor. He'd been much the same in class; him and Luc (who I'd been subtly watching) had even gotten into it a little over darkroom slots. It was all very unlike his usual smiley self.

"Hey?"

Oliver nods. "Have you seen Kitan today?"

My stomach squirms. "No."

He sighs, visibly deflating. "I really need to talk to her. I guess I can try again with Sarah, but I think she's getting pretty annoyed. So, and I mean this in the kindest way, you're sort of my last resort."

Oliver and I have never really been close, though things are typically cool between us. He knows that Kitan and I don't hang out, so things must be dire if he's coming to *me* for help concerning her.

"We're not going to the ball together anymore." He sighs again. "The Polaroids. Something came out. I did something that I wish I could take back—but it's a misunderstanding. She doesn't want to talk to me, and I don't want to pressure her, so I'm staying away. But I need her to know that I can explain. Will you tell her that?"

I process this new information with what I know already.

This means that Kitan didn't release the Polaroids. I didn't think she did, but this confirms it.

Still. Her behavior in the meeting yesterday—ignoring me, staying quiet the whole time.

Does she think that I did this?

I bristle with frustration.

Kitan will definitely be at the assembly, maybe I can corner her. We are overdue for another chat. "Okay," I say, and Oliver's eyes spark with hope. "I'll tell her."

"Thanks, Iyanu."

Then he rushes off, waving to Navin as he passes my locker.

"What did he want?" Navin asks when I join him, linking our arms as we start down the hallway.

"Turns out him and Kitan aren't going to the ball together anymore."

Navin startles. "What? Why?"

"The Polaroids."

The grim expression on his face echoes the heaviness I feel.

Mr. Leighton has yet to arrive at Lord Ardley Hall when we get there, but practically everyone else has; their overlapping conversations fill up the grand room as they mingle between the assembled Louis chairs.

Navin and I weave through the crowd looking around for Kitan, and I eventually spot her over by the French doors, the gold highlights in her hair shining in the afternoon sunlight. She's sitting with Sarah and Heather, Marcus and the rest of the rugby lads to their right. Quincy, who keeps glancing forlornly over at Heather and his brother, sits with Jordan in the same row. But the other players fill the seats between them, making their stark fracture even more pronounced.

Luc is nowhere in sight.

The rugby lads are joking around, and as Kitan sits there smiling at whatever is being said, I almost feel bad about interrupting her fun.

"Okay. I'm going in," I say, squaring my shoulders.

"You got this," Navin says.

Summoning the determination of my inner Yorùbá mother, I head toward the group. Kitan notices my approach first, her laughter morphing into a confused frown, but then she recognizes the look in my eyes and her expression turns to dread. She knows what's coming next.

I weave through the chairs before stopping in the row in front of her. The others are all staring at me now, mostly with confused expressions, but Heather's annoying smirk is firmly in place.

I ignore her.

"Óyá, Oreoluwakitan. Let's go," I say, switching to my Yorùbá accent.

The uncertainty in her eyes switches to anger and I can feel the discomfort practically oozing from her tense shoulders.

Heather chuckles, but I ignore her again.

"Let's. Go."

Kitan holds my gaze, and for a second I think that perhaps my tactic won't work, that she'll brush me off again in front of everyone. But then she huffs, gets up, and storms out the French doors. I follow her into the perfectly manicured garden, shutting the doors behind me.

I barely have enough time to gather my bearings in the cold air before she rounds on me.

"Why would you cause such a scene?" she whisper-shouts.

I put on an innocent affectation. "Oh, I didn't realize, my apologies!"

Kitan starts to retort, but hesitates, glancing over my shoulder at her friends who are probably watching our exchange.

I scoff. "What the hell is going on, Kitan? Which one of your friends sent out the Polaroids?"

The heat in Kitan's eyes flares, and she stuffs a hand into the inside pocket of her blazer, shoving something into my chest.

Her Polaroid.

The photo I took at the exact moment Oliver chose her. Luc and Oliver stand out of focus in the foreground like sentinels on either side of her shining light—her large smile and dancing eyes captured in time.

I glance up at her now glossy eyes, at her jaw clenched with the effort of holding back the tears, then back down at the Polaroid as I turn it over.

Oliver is only going to the ball with you because of a bet.

Dread washes over me, and I meet her eyes again as she wipes a tear that escapes.

She chuckles humorlessly. "It was all just a bet he made with one of the rugby guys. I don't know who, but I guess I was silly enough to think he'd actually want me, right?" She grabs the Polaroid back, tucking it into her blazer pocket again. "My friends wouldn't do this to me."

The way she says it.

I clutch at my camera strap. "There's no way you think I did this."

"'Let's all make a fool out of Kitan,'" she continues, as though I didn't speak, glancing away to the bed of snowdrops, crystal white in the sunlight despite the cold weather. "'She's always deluded enough to think that *this time* she'll be the one.'"

Her voice cracks, and she closes her eyes, taking a breath. After a moment, her tired eyes meet mine again.

"It doesn't matter what I think, Iyanu," she whispers. "Everyone else thinks you did it. And I really just can't do this right now. I'm sorry."

She hurries past me, but freezes, staring through the French doors into the hall. The alarm in her expression sends me running over to see what's happening.

Sprawled out on the floor with the chairs scattered and upturned around them, Luc and Jordan are scrambling, grabbing, *punching* at each other.

"Oh my God," Kitan says.

I yank the doors open to the loud jeers and chanting of the watching crowd.

Jordan is on top, his larger stature over the blond giving him the advantage. But then Luc jabs at his leg, just above the cast, and he falls with a harsh grunt. Luc quickly scrambles on top of him.

Kitan takes off, presumably to find Sarah and Heather, and I quickly scan the crowd for Quincy before I even realize it's what I'm doing.

I find him standing on the other side of the circle of onlookers, the pained expression on his face telling me that he's trying to calculate the best way to jump into the fight and stop it. Marcus stands next to him, looking completely at a loss for what to do as he shakes his brother's shoulder frantically.

Heart racing, I quickly squeeze my way into the mob toward him, but stumble when I catch a snippet of someone's conversation.

". . . this is about the whole gay thing, isn't it? Has Jordan really been faking it?"

I turn this way and that, trying to find the source of the absurd comment.

"That's what his Polaroid said."

The words come from behind me, but there are just way too many people around to spot them.

It's nonsense. People don't go around pretending to be marginalized for imaginary brownie points.

Well, except maybe Heather.

"Iyanu!"

The appearance of Navin through the crowd jolts me out of my thoughts.

"What the hell happened?" I shout. Unlike Marcus, who's always happy to be in the spotlight, Jordan is very much the laid-back twin. He does not get into fights. "And what's all this rubbish people are saying about Jordan?"

But before Navin can respond, there's another swell of noise, drawing our gazes back to the fight. Quincy has joined the fray, trying to pull Jordan out from underneath Luc while simultaneously pushing the blond away.

"Should I help?" Before I can stop Navin, he jumps in too, pulling at the back of Luc's jumper, dodging the swinging elbows.

And then Mr. Leighton arrives with Mr. Roberts, the caretaker, rushing in behind him. The crowd parts to let them through and Mr. Roberts, tall and built, lifts Luc off Jordan in one smooth motion. Jordan stumbles to his feet, ready to advance on Luc again, but Quincy holds him back.

For a few long moments the entire hall is silent.

"What on earth is going on in here?" Mr. Leighton, normally hard to ruffle, is bright red with rage.

Both Luc and Jordan start speaking at the same time, but the graying man holds up a hand, silencing them instantly. "Both of you. My office." Neither of them move. "Now!"

Luc jolts into action, grumbling under his breath in French and shoving his way through the crowd. Jordan tries to leave too, but he stumbles again, and Quincy catches him before he can hit the ground. Navin quickly grabs the crutches sprawled a few feet away from them and hands the pair to Quincy.

"Now"—all our heads turn back to Mr. Leighton—"clean this place up."

The words send everyone into motion, picking up chairs and identifying their scattered belongings. But I stand unmoving, the realization of what just happened settling like a rock in my stomach.

I glance over to Heather, who's now holding on to Marcus's arm, a faux worried expression on her face. Kitan and Sarah are next to them, whispering to each other . . .

I can't do this on my own.

To figure out who stole my negatives, I need to find out what could have possibly happened to spur one of them to expose everyone's secrets and create an atmosphere so toxic that it could lead to this. But what I've just witnessed tells me I'm already in over my head.

I glance over to where Navin is still rooted to the spot in the center of the room, taking in his frightened eyes staring at the crimson drops on the floor from Luc's gushing nose and Jordan's bleeding brow.

Navin had been through this before at his old school. Lies, secrets, rumors, fights . . . That's why he's here at Wodebury in the first place.

I can't drag him into this sort of mess again.

Watching Quincy's retreating back, I make my decision and hurry out the hall to catch up. "Q!"

Quincy pauses, glancing over his shoulder. "Yaya?"

"I'm good from here," Jordan says, taking the crutches and continuing on up the hallway.

"You sure?"

But the twin just waves without looking and disappears around the corner.

Quincy turns to me. "You okay?"

"Let's do this," I say, holding his gaze. "Let's find out who did this together."

Naturally, the assembly doesn't go ahead, but the heavy feeling that's now replaced my nerves about it is somehow worse.

Navin and I meet up in the east wing after fourth period to walk together to English Literature—our final class of the day and the only one all of us on the committee have together.

Luc and Jordan's absence will definitely be felt.

"All right, everyone, grab one of these and take your seats," Mrs. Tarar says, placing two stacks of paperbacks at opposite sides of the room as we all file in.

Unlike the other class Mrs. Tarar teaches—there are only seven of us in photography—English Lit is one of those A level courses that's always hugely popular, and so takes place in one of the lower year's amphitheater style classrooms with enough space to fit all twenty-seven of us in this group. The wooden school desks that line each row have those lids you can open like a pizza box to store your notebooks inside, and the nostalgia eases the heaviness a little.

Starting up the closest aisle, Navin and I head to our usual seats at the end of one of the middle rows, both of us grabbing a copy of the text as we walk by.

A Midsummer Night's Dream.

There are so many things wrong with Shakespeare's plays. That much I'd learned from having read them all and watching adaptations that had *tried* to rectify the problematic elements. But the first English Lit exam at the end of the year would be testing us on one of them, so here we are. We'd finished *Romeo and Juliet* last week, and I was definitely ready to move on to a comedy.

Navin groans as we sit down.

I chuckle. "Sorry, love."

He groans again. "When will this end? I don't think I can do this anymore."

"Don't worry, we'll survive it."

He raises a brow. "Of course you'd say that, 'Little Miss I've read them all already because I've read every book ever.'"

I grin. "Why did you even bother choosing Lit if you were going to hate it so much?"

He clutches at his chest in mock outrage. "Hate—such a strong word!" Then he shrugs. "I'm a poet. Watch out, next term I'll be so on top of this class."

I chuckle at his self-satisfied smirk, then turn to the front where Mrs. Tarar is calling for the class's attention.

"So," she says, clapping her hands together. "*A Midsummer Night's Dream.* Has anyone read it before? Who can give a quick summary?"

"I've read it, Miss," Heather says.

We all turn to her, but she quirks an eyebrow directly at me as if to say "What of it?"

I don't bother to hide my eye roll.

"Brilliant," Mrs. Tarar says, gesturing for Heather to continue.

"Well, there's a fairy called Puck. And one day, when all the human characters end up in the woods, the fairy king tasks him with casting love magic on them because he saw one of the pairs arguing. But Puck accidentally spells the wrong people. So they end up falling for the wrong partners, and things go south." She shrugs, glancing around the room. "A lot more happens, but mostly it's all just yearning and unrequited love."

Mrs. Tarar nods. "Exactly. The story is essentially about the hijinks that ensue when we're dealing with love." She turns to the class as a whole. "Now, there are many sayings in the Western lexicon that can be attributed to Shakespeare. *The Merchant of Venice*'s 'All that glitters is not gold,' and 'We have seen better days' from *As You Like It*. But many Shakespearean sayings concern matters of the heart, two of the most popular ones coming from *Midsummer*. Does anyone know what they are?"

There's complete silence, but I know exactly which ones she's referring to. My gaze moves automatically to Quincy, who's sitting in the row below. He's already looking at me, a smirk on his face, and I know he's also thinking about our Shakespeare movie marathon.

My lips quirk at the challenge in his eyes.

Ready?

Grinning, Quincy turns to Mrs. Tarar, but I speak before he can. "'The course of true love never did run smooth.'"

Quincy turns back to me, an exaggerated expression of betrayal on his face. He quickly gathers himself and continues. "And the other one is 'Love is blind.'"

Heather scoffs, glaring at the both of us, but I can't bring myself to care. The twinkle in Mrs. Tarar's eyes tells me that she's loving our back-and-forth, and I bubble up with excitement.

Quincy isn't wrong, but he isn't completely right either. "Love is blind" is a Shakespeare quote, but that version is from another play.

"The full quote, Quincy?" Mrs. Tarar asks.

"Well, umm, there's the one in *The Merchant of Venice*. But you have the same sentiment echoed in *Midsummer* . . . Something about Cupid . . ."

I can't contain my grin, and Quincy notices. *Don't you dare,* he mouths.

Usually I'm nothing if not merciful, but this is just too fun. "'Love looks not with the eyes, but with the mind. And therefore is winged Cupid painted blind.'"

Friday 3:43 P.M.

Q

i'll get you next time

we'll see

lool want to meet up this evening and strategize next moves for our investigation?

lol okay sherlock

ha ha you're the worst

should we meet up at mine? mum's taking jordan to the hospital to make sure he's good after the fight and i said i'd go with

cool, mum's got the book club tonight so i'll just ride with her

how is jordan anyway?

they both got a "slap on the wrist." we've got a game on saturday against Stanhope so there's no way mr leighton was gonna suspend Luc. and jordan didn't start the fight.

i thought i was gonna have a heart attack when i saw them fighting

same tbh. but he's okay ☺

ELEVEN

Kitan

I'm packing my hair into a low bun for my violin practice when Heather and Sarah burst into my room unannounced.

Sighing, I move to my bed and turn off the song blasting from my phone. I really don't want to turn it off, because ever since I came to Wodebury, Afrobeat playlists quickly became my favorite thing to distract myself from my thoughts—and the message from my Polaroid won't stop spinning in my head.

When I turn around, Heather's settled down on the stool in front of the dressing table that I just vacated, eyes glued to her phone.

I let out a tired breath, looking at Sarah. She's sitting on my bed with her back against the carved headboard, and it's hard to miss the rigidness to her posture.

I glance at Heather, then back to Sarah again.

Something's clearly just happened.

Sarah notices my realization, but she shakes her head subtly, so I decide to leave it. She'll tell me about it later.

"So," I start, perching on the foot of the bed opposite the mirror. "What's up? I have to head to the music center soon."

And thankfully, Oliver won't be there.

"We were just talking about Career Day tomorrow," Sarah says. "About our outfits."

I meet her gaze in the mirror, and the hesitation in her eyes makes my skin prickle.

"Yeah?"

"I heard back from my stylist," Heather says. "Turns out Paula did get Beyoncé's yellow 'Hold Up' dress made in time."

I grit my teeth, securing the bun with a final hairpin, determinedly not thinking about my own Beyoncé outfit hanging in the wardrobe.

Just let it go.

"Right."

A brief silence.

Nope.

"I thought you wanted to be Angelina Jolie when you were younger."

Heather, eyes still focused on whatever conversation is happening on her phone, just shrugs. "Well, I wanted to be Beyoncé when I was a kid too so . . ." She shrugs again. "You're wearing her Beychella look anyway and they're totally different, so it won't matter. We all just want to look good, so no one's really going to be sticking to the rules that closely. No one knows for sure what or who we wanted to be growing up anyway." She chuckles and I can't tell if it's because of her joke or whatever was said on her phone.

"Yeah . . . ," I say, and my smile comes out more like a grimace, but Heather isn't looking anyway.

It doesn't matter. It really doesn't. This could even be a good thing. If we're both dressed as Beyoncé tomorrow, people will think about that instead of this whole Oliver situation.

I meet Sarah's gaze in the mirror again. She rolls her eyes at Heather's back and I cover up my chuckle with a cough, grabbing a toothbrush from my jar of combs to lay down my edges. Just as the cool gel touches my crown, Heather speaks again.

"So!" she starts, setting her phone down on the dressing table, her smile suddenly wide. "I was talking to my mum last night, and we have to decide now where we want to go for our summer trip with the guys, so she can set everything up."

I glance at my phone. "I have to leave for violin. Can we sort this out later?"

"Come on, pleeease," Heather says. "It'll be suuuper quick."

This is the Heather that keeps the three of us glued together, doe-eyed and excitable. We'd all started going on holidays together just months after Heather came to Wodebury. Most of the time it was just the three of us, but sometimes the guys would join too. Trips all over the place. One Christmas break, we were skiing at Val-d'Isère, and Luc, Jordan, and Marcus were playing yet another one of their ridiculously dangerous games on the slopes, which thankfully didn't land them in the hospital, but did get them kicked out of the resort. We'd had to spend the rest of the trip in Luc's winter place in Chambéry.

This is good. If we're all still going on holiday, then this Polaroid situation hasn't ruined everything. Things will be fine.

I quickly finish off the last swoop of my baby hairs, then settle down on the end of the bed with an exaggerated sigh. "Okay."

Heather squeals and Sarah grins, shuffling over to join us.

"So, we've got either Prague or Tenerife," Heather starts, listing them off on her fingers. "But Marcus was saying that if we do the whole 'sun, sea, and sand' thing then we should go to Mykonos instead of Tenerife." Then she scoffs. "Plus, Luc loves Mykonos. If we tell him we're going there, maybe he'll stop acting like a child and start hanging with us again. We can't have people continue to think our group is falling apart."

Luc finding out from his Polaroid that his former relationship with Heather wasn't real and being upset about it doesn't really read to me as "acting like a child."

"Mykonos then I suppose," I say, pulling on my boots in slight annoyance. I guess Marcus had the time to talk to Heather about holidays, yet texted to reschedule our conversation.

Sarah nods. "I agree."

"Perfect! I need a new tan," Heather says, turning to look in the mirror and grazing her fingers along her neck. It's slightly paler than the rest of her face. "I managed to land that huge brand deal I've been talking about." She pauses for dramatic effect. "Gabriel Towne."

Sarah and I gasp. "No way," we both say in unison.

Gabriel Towne is the European luxury beauty brand that Heather has been trying to collaborate with for months. They'd gotten really huge after a viral video from New York Fashion Week, and all the big beauty bloggers have apparently been trying to get a contract.

"Yes way!"

Heather grabs her phone, showing us the email from the brand, and scrolling down to the photos of the swag box from the upcoming collection. There's tons of makeup with the familiar gold casings embossed with the "GT" logo, and a matching jewelry set with a gold bracelet, necklace, and earrings, all encrusted with delicate sapphires.

"Basically, they're hoping to do this diversity thing in their next campaign. I'm so excited."

My smile disappears as a flash of anger surges through me.

I quickly file the emotion away and clear my throat. "A diversity thing?"

"Yeah, they said they wanted different marginal communities. And I'm a woman so obviously I contacted them. I deal with misogyny on my page every day."

Sarah and I share a look.

Does the brand know she's white? Because "marginal communities" is pretty broad, they *could* be including white women talking about their experiences of misogyny. But Heather doesn't look very white right now. Do they think they've added a woman of color to their campaign to talk about her intersectional experiences? Would they care either way? If they knew about Heather, would they have hired an actual Black woman instead?

My frantic thoughts are interrupted by Heather's phone buzzing.

"One sec." She leans back against the dressing table, thumbs flying across the screen, and I let out a tired sigh.

What could I even do about it?

Reaching forward to grab a spare hairband from the glass jar by the mirror, I briefly catch sight of Heather's phone screen in the reflection. But before I can really make sense of it, she leaps to her feet.

"Okay, so Marcus just texted me," she says, and the look she throws Sarah is just casual enough to appear innocent. "I'm going to film something for my channel."

We both watch in confusion as Heather pulls open the door.

"We'll continue the holiday stuff later."

And then she's gone.

I turn to Sarah, barely concealing my feeling of whiplash. If Heather was just going to rush off and have us figure this out later, I could have already left for my practice session.

But Sarah just shrugs, and I can't help but think about our conversation at breakfast this morning, her forced nonchalance at the whole Heather and Marcus situation.

"I guess that's that then," she starts, standing and opening the door to my room. "Come on, you need to get to practice and I need to prepare for the head girl workshop tomorrow."

I grab my violin case, then pull on my peacoat, and we make our way out of my dorm block. And it's then that I realize what I saw on Heather's phone. A text conversation with Luc's name at the top of the screen.

Why would she say it was Marcus?

I let out another sigh as we step out into the winter chill, and Sarah's despondent expression in the light of the slowly setting sun is answer enough to that question.

"I'll see you later, Kitan," she says, starting off across the courtyard. "Have a good practice."

I head in the opposite direction, the message from the Polaroid like a broken record playing over and over in my mind.

The discordant note I've just played echoes in the otherwise silent practice room, bouncing between the ceiling to the hardwood floor in a way that makes the walls feel like they are closing in.

Instead of throwing my violin across the room, I grip the neck tightly in my fist. The motion makes my raw fingers throb.

Calm. Breathe.

But the broken record in my head won't stop spinning, and I squeeze my eyes shut against the onslaught.

I thought I could handle being in here. It's just a practice room. Four walls steeped in the scent of dusty sheet music books. But even though I'm alone in the slowly darkening space as the sun sets, Oliver might as well be right next to me. Everything about the last time we were in here, everything about *every* time we've been in here, floods my mind.

Except how to play this duet.

The notes keep getting replaced by those words, throwing off the rhythm, shortening the chords, fumbling the fingering, scratching the bow—

Calm. Breathe.

The lingering scent of rosin from my violin case fills my nostrils, and when I finally open my eyes again, I catch a glimpse of myself in the mirror on the opposite wall: the sweat on my brow and tenseness of my jaw.

It's just an off practice. It's fine. These things happen.

Letting out a long sigh, I rearrange the sheet music on the metal stand in front of me.

"Bach will not be the end of me. Bach will not be the end of me. Bach will not be—"

The mantra is interrupted by a knock at the door, and Mrs. Hugo's pale face appears in the glass window. She smiles before letting herself in, and I automatically return the expression.

"I was just getting a bit of practice in. The Bach piece."

It's almost dinnertime. Mrs. Hugo must have been on her way out when she'd heard my playing. Hopefully not too much of it. She's wrapped up in a thick wool coat, and her long gray hair is let down in waves instead of its usual tight bun.

"Of course," she says, German accent heavy as she nods distractedly. Clearly, she'd come here to discuss something else. "I've just been on the phone with Mr. Leighton. You know about the fundraiser on Thursday evening?"

I nod slowly, wondering where this is going. With Wodebury's three-hundredth anniversary coming up in ten years, the school has started a massive project to revamp many of the buildings. To the surprise of no one they started with the sports facilities, and Thursday night is one of the many donor fundraising events capitalizing on the excitement of the rugby Away game with Stanhope over the weekend.

"Well," Mrs. Hugo continues with a smile. "He's asked if the orchestra can do a short performance for the guests and donors."

My heart quickens.

"Would you be open to doing the Bach piece? I spoke to Oliver already. He said he's fine with it if you are."

I can only imagine the expression on my face, so it's no surprise Mrs. Hugo quickly carries on. "We can always do one of the concertos from last season."

"No, it's fine," I say, nodding as convincingly as I can. I'm leader of the first violin section. This is what I do.

Her smile returns.

"Brilliant." She turns to leave, but then pauses. "Take a break, Kitan. Let your fingers rest. It wouldn't do to overwork yourself, especially before a performance."

My fingers throb again in support of the sentiment.

"Okay."

And with that, Mrs. Hugo heads on her way.

We can just play together. We don't have to talk.

I take my time packing away the violin, running my fingers along the tiger-like stripes in the wood on the back of the instrument, a sour feeling in the pit of my stomach.

It's fine.

Heading out of the music center, I follow the lit path back to Lady Chalford, gripping hard at the handle of the case to focus on something other than the tears burning behind my eyes.

Then Mum's ringtone buzzes in my pocket and I quickly answer it.

"Good evening," I say softly, switching to my Yorùbá accent. Unfortunately, the signs of my impending breakdown bleed through, and Mum recognizes them instantly.

"Oyin, what's wrong?"

She's the only one who calls me by that middle name, and the tone of her voice brings the tears spilling out of me. I recount everything that happened in the practice, from repeatedly messing up the fingering to Mrs. Hugo's request.

Playing music comes right from the center of your emotions, and that's especially true for the violin. Oliver and I had built this performance together. Our friendship grew out of it, and I'd been channeling all that into my performance.

Now the words from the Polaroid won't stop plaguing my mind.

I don't say any of that to Mum though.

"It's already wild that Mrs. Hugo made me leader of the first violin section. I'm the only Black girl in orchestra and I got it. But today I just kept messing up. Over and over." I take a shuddering breath. "It's like I'm just sh-showing all the reasons why she shouldn't have."

Mum sighs. "Má sọ̀rọ̀ bẹ́ẹ̀. It'll be okay. One bad practice won't ruin everything."

I turn the corner onto the short cobblestone path leading up to the lake. There will be more people around on the other side of it, so I pause at the foot of the bridge. "Okay."

I try to believe her words. I really do.

"Try and wind down. Read a book or go and see Iyanu or something. Try to take your mind off it."

That muddled mix of emotions returns at the mention of Iyanu. "I'll try."

"Okay, dear."

I steer Mum back to whatever reason she'd originally called, filling me in on all the gist about the ówàmbẹ̀s happening in Lagos this weekend, but let my thoughts wander as I stare out at the water.

Oliver had made the bet with one of the rugby guys, and that was bad enough. But now everyone knows because of the Polaroids, and they're all treating me differently. That random girl in the breakfast queue never would have talked to me like that before, the rugby players only sticking around when Heather is with us wouldn't be the case, and the whole group basically falling apart never would have happened. I've worked too hard and sacrificed too much to get the position I have here. Heather was right earlier. The group has to be a unit, otherwise what was the point of everything?

It's been barely two days since the Polaroids came out and they're already changing me. Breakfast this morning shouldn't have been such a mess. I should be doing what I've always done: finding out what I need to know to guide my own actions, instead of letting this message control me. If I was doing that, I'd already know what's going on with Jordan. And Luc. And everyone.

And everything about the bet.

Mum says something about one aunty and the colors of the aṣọ-ẹbí, and I hum absentmindedly.

Why did Oliver make the bet in the first place? And if Iyanu released the Polaroids, why would Oliver have told her about it? It would have been in his best interest to keep it a secret. And either way, I'm never speaking to him again, much less to ask him about this.

But who did he make the bet with?

The not knowing is the problem. Not understanding how everything could shift so significantly after one weekend.

I need to find out. That's my starting point to get everything back in order again.

Tuesday 6:17 P.M.

> don't think I haven't noticed you're avoiding me Marcus

TWELVE

Iyanu

Mum calling me down to the car is a saving grace from staring at the blank Word document that's supposed to become my *WeCreate* article. But my thoughts are still there even as I strap myself into the passenger seat.

I'd hoped I could get started on it without having the photos from the fair to look at, even just a brief outline.

But that's just not how photo articles work.

A few minutes into our journey to the Villars', Mum cuts into my worried musings. "Did you use all my red yarn?"

Her gaze is focused on the road ahead, which is lucky because my eyes widen briefly in panic. I thought I'd have more time before she noticed it was missing. It's not like I can tell her that I've become an amateur private investigator who used the rest of her red yarn to put together a murder board of the scanned Polaroid printouts when I should have been working on my article. A murder board that is now hidden underneath my bed.

"It's for a . . . project that I'm doing with Quincy."

It's not exactly a lie. In fact, it's basically the truth.

Before I can pat myself on the back for my quick thinking, she continues. "Oh, for Lit class? Is that why you're meeting up tonight?"

I brush away some nonexistent lint from my jeans. "We're reading *Midsummer* in Lit."

Again, true. But it doesn't answer her question.

Luckily, she doesn't notice.

"I'm glad you and Quincy are talking properly again. When I told Claudia that you were coming today because you two were meeting up, she was so excited. Apparently, he spent hours cleaning his room."

I quickly capitalize on this new opening to steer the conversation away from me and any more almost-lies. "Were you able to finish reading the pick for this month?"

"Finished it last night! It was so good. I tell you, I was even reading it on breaks during my shifts."

I chuckle. "Well, the rest of the ladies will be pleased."

"Oh, definitely. Especially Claudia," she says, rolling her eyes good-naturedly. "She's been moaning that I don't 'take enough time for myself' because I didn't finish the last three books."

It's true though. Mum doesn't take enough time for herself, but at least she has the book club. She and Quincy's mum have been best friends since they were undergrads. They'd started the book club together as a safe space for them and the few other Black women in nursing and medi-cine courses. They'd kept it going ever since, and now, living in a town as white as this, it serves the same purpose. Even when Tia Claudia moved back to Cuba for a few years after uni—where she got married and had the boys—they had the sessions over the phone.

I wish I had something similar with Kitan and the few other Black girls at Wodebury. A space away from the stifling whiteness. But then I remember who I am and what things are like with Kitan.

At least I have WeCreate.

The rest of the journey is spent with the quiet sound of Mum's Naij playlist filling the car, her soft humming lulling me back to calmness.

But when we pull into the Villars' driveway, a heavy melancholy set-tles back in my stomach at the sight of the massive stone cottage lit up with garden lights.

It's changed a bit since the last time I was here, but in a lot of ways, it's the same. The front door's been repainted ivy green from the previous navy blue, but the same bronze knocker still sits shiny in the center. Bare wisteria branches waiting for spring to bloom climb higher up the building, but they still frame the doorway.

What's different are the big little things. The pebbled driveway and perfectly groomed flower beds are no longer littered with stray rugby gear, and three vintage bicycles don't rest against the side of the house. The brothers don't live here full-time anymore, not since they started boarding in Year Nine, and their absence only serves to heighten mine.

"You okay?"

Mum's voice startles me out of my reverie, dark brown eyes asking the other question she's not sure she should speak. *Can you handle it?*

I look away, grabbing my satchel from the floor by my feet. "I'm good. Let's go in."

Tia Claudia must have been waiting to hear us drive up, because when we step out of the car, the front door bursts open and a second later I'm wrapped up in her warmth.

"It's so good to see you." Her soft voice brushes lightly against my ear and I snuggle in closer as my heart swells. She must have been baking, because the guayabera she's wearing smells like sugar and berries. Tia Claudia's "take time for herself" is definitely cooking and baking, and she'd passed that love down to Quincy.

"It's good to see you too, tia."

She pulls away, warm hands moving to my cheeks, and she just … . looks at me. Her expression is warm, so I do the same, taking in the smile lines etched into her light brown skin; the excitement emanating from her large brown eyes, so like Quincy's; and the long dark curls that now flow past her shoulders.

I let out a breath, thick emotion welling in my throat.

Over the past three years, I'd seen her and Tio Félix at parents' evenings and a few Home rugby matches. But it was nothing like this. Nothing so up close. Nothing like standing in the Villars' driveway.

"So beautiful," she says, rubbing her thumbs over my baby hairs, and I just about keep it together.

"Me?" I croak out. "What about you?"

She grins, smacking my arm lightly. "Oh, stop it!"

The hem of the guayabera goes almost down to her knees, so it's probably one of Tio Félix's.

"Is tio around?"

"No, he's away on business till the weekend after next," she says wistfully, then takes my hand, pulling me toward the door.

Mum scoffs jokingly from behind us. "Oh, don't mind me, just here to clear the gutters."

Tia Claudia sends me a smirk before calling back over her shoulder. "The tools are in the shed out back, Dami."

My loud cackling joins the laughter coming from the living room as the three of us take off our shoes then head down the corridor. The interior is still exactly the same. Exposed oak beams, wood floor covered in soft woven carpets, and photos of Quincy and the twins lining the wall up the stairs.

All four of the other usual book club members are seated in a circle in the cozy living room, slouched low from their laughter on the squishy leather sofas. There are two empty spaces for Mum and Tia Claudia, and on the coffee table in the center is a large tray with mugs of tea, corned beef sandwiches, and blueberry oatmeal cookies.

The women all look up as we walk in. Mrs. Olarinde and her two grown daughters, Monilola and Jaiye, and Quincy's older cousin Tula.

The scene is so familiar that I can't believe I haven't seen it in so long.

Within seconds, I'm passed around the room in a blur of excitement and tight squeezing hugs before I find myself in the doorway again, the two empty spaces now filled.

"Just head on up, honey," Tia Claudia says, "Quincy's in his room."

"Cool, I'll . . ." But just as quickly as my five minutes of fame began, it disappears as they all settle back into conversation.

Chuckling, I leave the room and head up the stairs. The first-floor landing is shrouded in darkness, curtains and window shades shut tight, but it doesn't matter because I can make my way around this house in my sleep.

My heart pounds heavily as I inch slowly to Quincy's room at the end of the hall.

Standing in the open doorway is like stepping back in time, memories of our final argument flashing through my mind. Every biting word returning to me as I take in the socks strewn all over the floor, the warm scent of cinnamon in the air, the low hum of the projector rolling film credits onto the blank wall above the desk.

I peek around the room to find Quincy slouched against the headboard. It's dark in here too, only tiny slivers of moonlight fighting through the drawn curtains, but I can still see the headphones around his ears, his eyes focused on his phone.

I wave a hand to draw his attention.

When he looks up, recognition flashes in his eyes and he scrambles to his feet, pulling off the headphones.

"Hey! Sorry, I was just texting Heath—" He snaps his mouth shut, rethinking, but then realizes it's already obvious who he was going to say. "Heather."

I'm not entirely sure what to do with that because I wouldn't have thought anything of it if he hadn't acted so weird. Like there's a reason I shouldn't know he's texting her.

An awkward silence hangs in the air before I finally have to break it. "I thought your mum said you'd cleaned your room," I say, toeing at the *Black Panther* socks closest to the door.

He shrugs sheepishly. "I did. But I was looking for another pair of socks earlier. It might've been a sunny day, but it's still cold."

Unable to help myself, I eye the *Sesame Street* character on his socked feet. "And so, you decided on Cookie Monster? Well-known protector of humans from the perils of climate change?"

"Yup." He chuckles lightly. "He'll save us all."

More silence.

"Umm . . . you can come in?"

Despite the hesitation in his voice, I decide to take the plunge.

After stepping over the threshold, I cross the large room and settle on the desk chair, placing my satchel on the floor by my feet. The light from the projector warms my skin as the film credits scroll over my face. There's no sound coming from the speakers dotted around the room so he must have been in the middle of packing up whatever film he was watching when he got sidetracked by his phone.

By Heather.

Quincy's already looking at me when I turn back to him, the expression on his face a strange mixture of confusion and recognition. I'm unable to puzzle it out further because he's suddenly moving, turning off the projector and switching on the light.

The sudden brightness is jarring, but I quickly adjust.

"I'm going to head down and greet your mum. I'll be back in a sec."

I nod distractedly as he leaves, glancing around the familiar room. With most of his stuff now in his dorm at Wodebury, it's a little bare— only the dark wood furniture, still well-cared-for plants hanging from the beams above, and stacks of books by the bay window seat—but one sight stops me in my tracks.

On the bedside table is a six-segment collage frame, and each picture punches a hole inside me.

The photos are mine. Clunky and inexperienced, but still mine. They're from that week when our families went down to the beach in Devon. We were probably about eight or nine, but I remember it being a particularly hot summer. I'm only in one of the photos, the one Quincy took of me splashing in the sea.

It's unclear how long I stare at the pictures, but soon Quincy returns and I shake myself out of my thoughts.

"So, I made a murder board. Well, the beginnings of one."

Eyes lighting up, Quincy goes to sit in the bay window. "For real? Okay, Watson." I raise a brow and he laughs, the deep sound filling me up. "What? We can't *both* be Sherlock."

A smile tugs at my lips and I shake my head exasperatedly. "Mr. Leighton let me photocopy the Polaroids. At first, I was just going to study the messages, but then when I got home, I had the idea for the murder board. I'm thinking maybe we can start our 'investigation' there."

I wonder if I should bring up the fact that his friends are my main suspects, but my phone starts blowing up in my pocket.

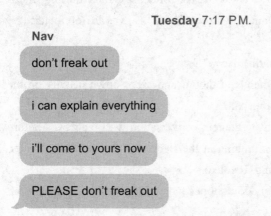

Tuesday 7:17 P.M.

Nav

don't freak out

i can explain everything

i'll come to yours now

PLEASE don't freak out

"What the hell." I look up from my phone in confusion, only to find Quincy glaring at his. He comes over, holding up the screen to me.

It's a post on Jordan's page from just five minutes ago. Navin and Jordan sit snuggled up in the bay window of Jordan's room, Navin's head tucked into Jordan's neck, the latter's gentle smile deepening the dimples in his cheeks.

The caption is a single red heart.

Suffice it to say, I'm freaking out. "What the hell is this?"

"That idiot."

I turn to Quincy. "What the hell is going on?"

But Quincy doesn't respond, instead he storms out the door and I hurry after him into Jordan's room.

"*This* is what you decide to do?" he yells at his brother. "What good is this going to do?"

Navin's eyes bug out, just as surprised to see me here, as he and Jordan hurry to their feet. They're standing at the bay window, dressed in the same clothes as the photo.

"I can explain," Navin says hurriedly, but my confusion has turned to plain old hurt.

"You guys are together? And I had to find out online*?*"

"No! It's not like that. It's not real," Jordan responds, turning frantically between me and Quincy, who scoffs, but my eyes are too focused on Navin's subtle flinch.

"Somebody explain this. Now," I say.

Quincy throws his hands in the air and drops down heavily on the bed, placing his head in his palms.

The sheepish pair have a silent conversation with their eyes before Navin turns back to me, tugging at the sleeve of his cashmere sweater. "We're not actually dating. It's fake."

The brothers probably don't notice the way Navin's voice changes on the last word, but I do.

"See, look." Navin carries on, grabbing something from Jordan's desk and handing it to me.

It's another Polaroid, Jordan leaning back against a tree in the clearing just before everyone started to arrive for the matchmaking event.

I quickly flip it over.

It's so obvious you're faking it.

I look up, glancing between Jordan and Navin.

Jordan crosses his arms, gritting his teeth. "Everyone saw it. They're all convinced that it's about me faking being queer this whole time 'cause I haven't dated anyone since I came out."

The words spark a memory of the whispered conversation I'd caught in the crowd when he and Luc were fighting. The accusation I couldn't understand.

I frown. "So you're trying to prove you're not faking being gay by . . . fake dating Navin?"

The responding silence is answer enough.

Quincy shifts closer to his brother, and even though Jordan is standing over him, there's way more power in the gentleness of the motion.

"You not wanting to date anyone is nobody's business, Jordan." He sighs. "But I told you I was going to handle it and get everyone to stop."

Jordan slumps back down on the bay window seat as all the fight leaves him, and Navin follows suit, hugging one of the cushions to his chest.

"You can't fight all my battles for me, Q. I—I just couldn't take it anymore," Jordan says, eyes shiny with moisture. "I *know* you two get that. People are always questioning and invalidating both of your queerness 'cause y-you're bi."

He's right. Cishet and queer folks alike.

"They're rumors, Jordie . . ."

And as Quincy says that, I'm momentarily taken back to Year Nine again, and it's too hard to listen to his words as he reassures his brother. Wishing the same words had been there for me when I had to deal with all the rumors.

I settle down on the other end of the bed as the earlier hurt seeps in a little deeper.

"I know, okay? I get it." Quincy continues, "And I'm sorry, but this is such a bad idea."

But the post is already out there.

"I had to do something," Jordan says, then holds Quincy's gaze knowingly. "Besides, other than you and Marcus, Luc was the only one who knew. He had to have been the one who sent out the Polaroids."

I perk up at that. "Is that why you two were fighting?"

What I thought was a simple question turns out to be the opposite, because Jordan stays silent for a moment, sending Quincy an unsteady look.

"Sort of, yeah," the twin finally says.

But the new sleuthing part of my mind has reawakened, trying to interpret the other conversation that seems to be happening between Jordan and his brother.

Luc was the only one who knew.

It doesn't make sense.

I speak before I can stop myself.

"But you *are* gay. So why do you think Luc released the Polaroids? What does Luc know that you're faking?"

Another difficult question apparently, so I turn to Navin, but the confusion in his eyes tells me he doesn't know either.

"I'm not really ready to answer that yet," Jordan whispers, and the vulnerability in his eyes feels so familiar.

"Okay." I nod, deciding easily not to push, and Jordan lets out a breath, thankful.

"I just need to do this right now and get everyone off my back."

I glance over at Navin. *This is a terrible idea.*

Navin answers with a pained looking shrug, and I soften a little.

Navin . . .

He pleads silently in response, brown eyes now a little glassy.

I sigh, turning back to Quincy just as he looks away from Jordan, apparently also having a silent conversation. He runs a hand over his messy plaits, staring at the floor, deep in thought.

"We should get them in on our plan," he says, meeting my eyes. "They might know stuff that we don't."

I recognize the truth in that, but still hesitate. "Not Navin. He doesn't need this."

The guy in question makes an indignant noise, drawing my gaze to his frowning face. "What's this? What don't I need?"

My eyes dart to Quincy. Jordan. Back to Navin.

"We're trying to . . ." But I'm not really sure how to explain it. This has all gotten away from my original plan.

I just want the Black Girls Winter Fair negatives back so I can write my article.

Noticing my discomfort, Quincy takes over. "Whoever released the Polaroids also stole Yaya's negative binder with really important photos for an article she's writing." He pauses, gesturing to Jordan's Polaroid. "So, not only because they're ruining our lives, but we also need to find out who did this so we can get them back."

Navin's frown deepens, eyes filling with hurt. "Why wouldn't you want me to help? You know I want you to get the *WeCreate* job. I pushed you to go for it."

"This could get messy, Nav," I whisper, then gesture between him and Jordan. At Jordan's black eye. "It already has."

I don't want you to get dragged into drama again and get hurt.

Understanding sparks in his eyes and there's a brief silence as Navin considers. Then he tucks a stray lock of hair that's escaped his bun back behind his ear and sits up straight. As I hold his gaze, all I find is resolve. "I want to help."

Even as I feel unsteady, my heart warms. "Okay."

"I want to help too," Jordan says, leaning forward. "I know Luc did this. We just need proof."

This seems to spark something in Quincy because he grins wide. "Iyanu has a murder board."

The look on their faces when I set up the murder board on the easel in my room is unexpected.

Navin's eyes devour the display. "This. Is. Amazing."

I smile with an awkward shrug. "Thanks. There's still a lot missing though."

"No . . . don't downplay this, Yaya."

Quincy's expression is so full of awe that I turn from the three of them sitting on my bed to take in the board myself.

I suppose it is pretty impressive. I'd taken a large corkboard from Dad's studio downstairs and pinned up all the scanned Polaroid printouts in a spiral, front and back to show the secret that went with each one. Some photos had more than one person in them, but whoever did this seemed to know who I'd made the subject of each shot, making it easy to label them with its recipient in the white space at the bottom of each Polaroid. It's both flattering of my skills and annoying, considering what they'd gone and used them for. Mr. Leighton had only managed to round up twenty-five in total, but they would have to do.

"These are the unsolved connections," I start, pointing to the multitude of red yarn strings connecting the photos to each other. "The yellow yarn means possible connections. The blue ones connect the people who are mentioned in each other's secrets, and green means solved connections . . . There aren't many of those."

The guys nod their understanding, and I grab a stack of Post-it notes from the dressing table. "I haven't put these up yet, but the pink Post-its will show that the person had the means to do it, and red Post-its will show that they had a definite motive."

Quincy points to the committee members' Polaroids arranged in a circle at the center of the spiral. Kitan's and Jordan's are random pictures from their socials that I'd printed out. All of them have orange Post-its next to them except for Navin's.

"And the orange Post-its here? What do they mean?"

Stalling, I write the message from Jordan's Polaroid on a scrap piece of white paper and pin it up next to his photo, just like I'd done with Kitan's, before turning back to them. I tug at my belt loop awkwardly. "Orange Post-its mean they have a possible motive . . . Those are my main suspects."

The three of them turn to me in unison, shock evident on their faces.

I hurry to continue. "No, not you guys. Not Marcus either. It's just— no one outside this circle would know these kinds of secrets about you lot. And only the committee knew I'd been given special permission to develop those photos over the weekend, so it has to be one of you."

Jordan pipes up. "Well, I know it's Luc. We just need to get some proof for Mr. Leighton, and he'll get Luc to give you back your negatives. Problem solved."

I hold in a sigh.

My instincts are screaming to me that it's Heather. She's the only one brazen enough to do something like this without fear of consequences. But the Polaroids ended things for her and Quincy with the ball, so that's hard to square with any reasonable motive.

And while there's clearly something more going on between Jordan and Luc, it's hard to see why it would be Luc. Aside from Kitan and the people in this room, he's the only other person I'd struggled to put an orange Post-it next to. Because judging by the meeting, the fight during the assembly, and the way Luc is rarely around them anymore, everyone seems to be angry with him. Why would he do something that would make everyone hate him?

But then again, Jordan knows Luc better than I do.

"What's his motive?" I ask.

Jordan chuckles, but there's no humor in it. "We've all been training towards the England team for forever. Hell," he says, gesturing to himself and Quincy, "us and Marcus started boarding because training really stepped up in Year Nine when we were all trying for county. We wanted to be closer to the field. Get more training, more practice. Live and breathe the stuff."

The way he says it, you can practically feel the exhaustion.

"When Luc and I made county, I became captain of our year's boys' team. Luc was cool about it, but I *know* he wanted it. Now we both want that one national spot that opened up. I'm benched right now 'cause I'm injured, but the message on my Polaroid . . . Luc is trying to get in my head."

Jordan's eyes glaze over in thought for a few moments before snapping back into focus. "Once I get back to playing, if I'm not at my best, I risk my standing with the other guys. And Mr. Forrester won't put me forward to try out for the national team. He's already been stalling Marcus because of everything that's going on with his panic attacks. Luc probably sent out all these lies on the Polaroids just to cover himself."

My eyes drift to Navin's. I know he's thinking about the message on his, so I send him a comforting smile.

"Iyanu, you said on the ride here that whoever did this understands the photography lab equipment and knew the importance of your negatives, right?" Jordan continues, and I nod. "Well, Luc does photography. He's in your class. He had motive *and* means."

Oh.

Something that feels a little too much like hope sparks in my chest.

I grab a pink Post-it note and stick it next to Luc's Polaroid. He now has more than anyone else up there.

"Plus," Jordan says, glancing over at Quincy, "he's the one with The Locker."

The way he says the word makes it sound like a proper noun.

I have to ask. "The Locker?"

Jordan looks to his brother, and the elder sighs, waving him on.

"It's pretty gross. There's this locker in the boys' changing room that's basically Luc's stash place. Even when we were close, I stayed clear of it."

Quincy snorts. "I've never seen it either. But Marcus said he saw inside once accidentally, and that it was enough to wanna stay away from it too. Apparently it's like . . . aggressively cishet."

"A lot of the guys use it to stash stuff," Jordan continues. "I already searched through Luc's dorm room, but I didn't find anything. So I was going to try and break into the locker tomorrow during the Year Twelve boys' rugby match with our Hanwood kids when Luc's distracted. The girls' team is playing with their Hanwood kids first, so during our match is the perfect time.

The Locker is full of all kinds of secrets. Maybe Luc even used what's in it to come up with the Polaroid messages. Your negatives could be stashed in there too."

My tentative hope turns to genuine excitement. "Could he really have done it?" I ask, looking between them.

Navin shrugs. "It checks out to me. Plus, we have to start somewhere."

"Quincy?" I ask, but the more I think about it, the more my brain latches on to the idea. This could be it. I've got eleven days until the *WeCreate* deadline, but this could be over as early as tomorrow.

We all watch as Quincy thinks, coming to a decision.

"You won't be able to do the break-in," he says to Jordan. "Whatever Luc's motives, you're still the captain. Everyone will notice you gone. I can't either because I'll be playing."

I deflate a little. "Neither can I. I'm taking photos of the match with Mrs. Tarar."

We all turn to Navin, who's confident smirk makes my smile widen again, relieved to see a return to his usual self.

"Guess I'll have to save the day then, shall I?"

*Q created the chat "Iyanu's Angels" with you,
Jordan, and Nav*

Q

figured we needed a virtual space to strategize too

Nav

great idea!

lool, what is this name?

Q

we're spies, i had to keep on theme

also, i rewatched a couple of mission
impossible films last night to prepare

Nav changed the group photo

Q

i fully approve of that picture

Nav

Q

honestly, who's keeping track of the win counter
because i would like to log a win for that man's
workout routine, i could stare at him all day

loool i bet you're drooling

Q

i actually prefer to call it looking respectfully

hahahahaha

Jordan

sigh

how is this my life?

THIRTEEN

Kitan

I'm wearing several layers of skin-tone tights under these Beyoncé shorts, but the Wodebury chapel is always cold regardless of the season, so it's a back and forth between what's currently causing me the most misery—the temperature, or my hyperawareness of Oliver's presence.

The Hanwood kids are excited though, their high-pitched voices bouncing off the arches as they explore the space. The music department had gotten fifteen Hanwood kids for Career Day. A broad mix of six- to nine-year-olds to be corralled by five of us Year Twelves under our music teacher's supervision. We'd started off the day choosing instruments and making music. Now we're doing a tour of all the places the orchestra performs, the chapel being the last stop. After this, we'll break for lunch, play some rugby, and then they'll head back to school.

It's largely been enjoyable but sitting here in the choir stand on the right side of the chapel, I can't stop sneaking glances at Oliver on the opposite side. I've been attempting to avoid looking at him all day, and so far, I've only been about 55 percent successful. I'd felt his eyes on me from time to time throughout the morning too. And once, when we walked past the practice rooms, we'd even made eye contact.

Before my gaze can drift toward him again, I focus on the congregation seats.

"Kitan?"

I turn to Hina, Mrs. Tarar's adorable nine-year-old daughter, who'd been attached to my side all day. Apparently, all her friends had chosen different subjects, and so she didn't want to be alone. Her energy is light and open, and with everything going on, I'm just as in need of her constant presence as she is of mine.

She's dressed up as an orchestra conductor with her long black hair pulled back in a braid. Unlike most of the other kids, who'd taken a minute to settle in before their excitement came out, Hina hit the ground running. Her playful precociousness echoed in her wide smile, while a gentle wisdom shone through in the deep concentration she'd applied as I'd talked her through the notes on the violin.

It was nice watching her and the other kids perform. To feel music in such a pure state.

Especially after yesterday's horrible practice.

"Yeah?"

The little girl cocks her head to the side, staring at me with that same still gaze before grinning cheekily. "Is that your boyfriend?"

I splutter for a moment, and Hina giggles.

"Wh-What? No. He's not. Why would you ask that?"

Hina's grin widens.

"How'd you know who I was talking about?" I have no response, so she continues. "I was just asking because he won't stop looking over here. It's been all day. You've been doing it too."

Hina looks over at him and I peek out from behind my hair.

Oliver is showing Paul, a little Black boy from Hanwood and one of the two six-year-olds who'd chosen music, how to properly pluck the strings of his violin. Paul is doing well for someone who can barely lift the thing, and I can't help but coo a little inside at the size of Oliver's much larger hand next to his.

Then I catch myself and quickly snatch my gaze away.

After waking from another nightmare last night, I'd spent the time until sunrise staring out at the lake with my thoughts turning. Trying to come up with a plan to find out which rugby guy made the bet with Oliver. In the end, bold but calculated action seemed to be the only way to go about this.

I have to talk to someone on the team. But it has to be a discreet pursuit. There can't be a repeat of yesterday.

If only Marcus would stop dodging me.

"Kitan," Hina says, poking me repeatedly in my side. I turn to her smiling face. "He's coming over here."

A quick burst of panic rushes through me as I turn back to the opposite stands, squeezing at the banister in front of me. Paul is rushing off to the other kids who're playing noisily with the organ, carefully balancing the helmet of his astronaut outfit under his arm.

But I don't hear any of that. Not with Oliver walking right toward me, caution in his gaze. He hesitates when he sees that I've noticed his approach, freezing midwalk, asking a question with his eyes.

I nod slowly, and he quickly crosses to join.

When he stops in front of me, he has to look up from his position at ground level, but he's close enough that the scent of his vanilla lotion is strong, and I have to steel myself.

"Hey."

I fix my gaze on the left shoulder epaulet of his pilot costume. "Hi."

"Sorry, I just wanted to ask about the performance tomorrow."

He scratches at his ear, and my eyes follow the motion of his dangling earrings before returning to his shoulder again.

I can feel his hand resting on the banister, too close to mine.

"I hope it's okay that I agreed to do it. Mrs. Hugo kind of cornered me."

"It's fine."

Hina shifts in her seat, clearly feeling the awkwardness in the air.

"So I was thinking—" But he cuts himself off and starts again. "I just thought maybe we could practice?"

I'd sensed that's where this was going, but I don't know how to respond.

This isn't fair. Being around Oliver shouldn't feel like this.

Biting the corner of my lip, I finally meet his gaze, and his eyes are pleading.

Bet aside, the disaster session yesterday is still fresh in my mind. "I don't think I want to do that," I respond quietly, wishing my voice sounded stronger.

Oliver lets out a shaky breath. "Yeah, okay. Sorry . . ."

I look down at his hand. Too far away from mine.

When I look up again, he steps back with a nod, then leaves to join our other classmates with the kids by the organ.

After a brief moment of silence, Hina speaks. "Well. That was a lot."

"Yeah."

I need to get to the bottom of this.

Pulling out my phone, I open up my text messages.

Wednesday 12:01 P.M.

we need to talk.

and you better not ignore me this time.

Marcus:

i'm sorry

yeah, yeah. can we meet at lunch?

139

can't, sorting some things out for Mr. Forrester

Marcus.

okay, we can meet after the game

good

FOURTEEN

Iyanu

I really could have just come to school as "me on a weekend" for Career Day. A cozy normcore outfit with my camera hanging around my neck. Photographer. Easy.

But last week, Navin had insisted that we go all out, and so after a web search of fictional photographers, we put together the perfect Andrew Garfield as Peter Parker outfit. My spare black frame glasses instead of my usual tortoiseshell, a khaki jacket over a blue T-shirt, a dark gray hoodie, and jeans.

So yeah . . . me on a weekend.

Navin had scoffed at that when we'd met up in the photography lab before first period, brushing off some nonexistent lint from his Prince *Purple Rain* jacket. It was then that I couldn't take it anymore, insisting that he give me a rundown on how he'd gotten himself mixed up in this whole Jordan mess.

Apparently, Navin had called Jordan after the fight to ask how he was doing. The twin had been on the verge of tears, distraught over how every-one was hounding him about the lie on his Polaroid. So Navin had come up with the fake-dating plan.

Despite everything though, it is exciting when Navin and I walk into the Sixth Form common room at lunch. As expected, everyone has pushed "what you wanted to be growing up" to the furthest extent, and so all the Year Twelves together in one place feels like some sort of comic convention. Turns out, when they were younger, many of our classmates wanted to be Marvel, *Star Trek*, and *Lord of the Rings* characters.

Dodging a couple of pirouetting ballerinas, we head over to a vacant spot in the corner by the bookcases. It provides a great vantage point of everyone milling around the large room with its teal floral wallpaper, brown leather chesterfield sofas, and light wood-paneled floors.

The comfy chaise longue we settle in is also the perfect respite from being on our feet all morning wrangling excitable Hanwood kids. *All teachers deserve a raise.*

Navin nudges me in the side. "Kitan looks amazing. That yellow is stunning on her."

Glancing around, I spot her sitting by the windows on the other side of the room with Sarah, who's come dressed as a barrister. I recognize Kitan's Beyoncé outfit instantly as the star's headline Coachella look. A bright yellow cropped hoodie, jean shorts, and sparkly silver tassel boots.

"Really amazing." I twist my fingers together, a sad echo of the feeling inside me, because I kind of wish I could just walk over and tell her myself.

"What's amazing?"

We turn from Kitan to find Jordan setting his crutches up against the bookcase. He drops down next to Navin, draping an arm over his shoulders.

Navin must have somehow forgotten about their arrangement because his eyes bulge open as Jordan tucks him closer into his side.

Or maybe it's just the sight of Jordan's huge arms in scrubs.

"H-Hey," Navin splutters out, and I do my best to hide a chuckle behind my hand.

Jordan doesn't seem to notice how flustered Navin is though, simply grinning wide in response, which probably doesn't help Navin's situation.

I decide to save him. "We're talking about Kitan's outfit."

Jordan nods. "Oh, one hundred percent agree. But she always looks gorgeous so I wouldn't expect anything less." Then he pauses, making a face. "But what Heather's gone and done? That's just a mess for way too many reasons."

The drama department is in a completely different wing from photography, so I haven't seen Heather at all today, which is always a great thing.

But just as I'm about to ask what Jordan means, Quincy joins us.

"Afternoon, agents. We all set for The Locker break-in mission?"

But it's hard to focus on his words because . . .

"What the hell is going on here?" Navin asks, gesturing to Quincy's outfit.

The outfit mostly makes sense. Thanks to Tia Claudia passing down her passion for cooking and baking, he's always wanted to be a professional chef. So the white double-breasted jacket and tall chef's hat completely check out. What's utterly confusing though, is the nose and whiskers he's drawn on his face in what is likely eyeliner.

Quincy laughs, dropping down in the wingback in front of us. "Remy the chef!" At my and Navin's blank stares he just laughs again. "From *Ratatouille*!"

There's a beat of silence, and then we all fall into hysterics. Belly aching laughter that has me doubling over.

"I actually can't!" Navin says, trying to breathe.

Wheezing, I wipe the tears from my eyes. "Why are you like this? *Of course* you went with the rat instead of the other main character in the film! You know, an actual human?"

"Always gotta shake things up," Quincy responds, slouching low in the chair. "Plus, he was the better chef."

"You're ridiculous."

Quincy's eyes shine brightly with an almost childlike joy, and it's like no time has passed at all.

Then Navin nudges me in the side again, and I quickly look away.

"So . . ." I start, ignoring the feel of Quincy's gaze as I turn to Jordan.

"I know you chose biology today, and like, you're not playing. But I thought you'd just wear your rugby kit. Or maybe even the England one?"

All the other rugby guys I'd seen today, save Quincy, had worn theirs, including Luc—who I'd watched closely all morning in photography, but is nowhere to be found now. Considering all their aspirations and the game they'd be playing with the kids after lunch, wearing that seems to have been decided as the convenient choice.

Jordan just shrugs, but Quincy laughs. "Yeah, but when we were kids, Jordie was basically obsessed with Mum's job. He could barely even say the word 'anesthesiologist,' but he was convinced he was going to be one just like her."

"Whatever," Jordan huffs, kicking his brother's foot playfully.

Quincy rolls his eyes. "So everyone knows their objectives for the heist, affirmative?"

There's a beat of silence, and then we all fall into hysterics again.

Quincy can always be counted on to be a total nerd.

"Yeah, we got it," I say, but my words are cut off by Navin sitting up hurriedly and nudging me repeatedly in the side.

"Oh my God."

I turn quickly in the direction he's staring.

Heather and Marcus have just walked in, and the sight sends anger flaring so quickly through my system that I could throw up.

Much like the other rugby guys, Marcus is decked out in his rugby kit. But Heather . . . Heather has also come dressed as Beyoncé. Specifically, "Hold Up" Beyoncé, in a long ruffled yellow dress and a baseball bat in hand.

The dress itself is gorgeous and must have cost a fortune, which is nothing for most of the kids at Wodebury, and likely just spare change for the daughter of an earl.

But Heather herself . . . Heather is in blackface.

Navin and I turn to each other with identical open-mouthed stares before turning back to her. "Jesus Christ, Mary, and Joseph," he whispers.

Dressing up as Beyoncé is fine. Wanting to be Beyoncé when you grow up is pretty much everyone's dream. What's not fine is the fact that Heather is *so* bronzed (clearly, she'd pulled out all her bottles of fake tan and brown shade foundation last night) that it blows way past her usual blackfishing.

"I don't know what to say," Navin continues.

"Me neither."

I turn back to Quincy at his words.

He looks just as shocked as Navin and me, and I realize that being in the food tech lab today meant that he probably hadn't seen Heather all morning either.

"What do we do?" Navin asks, eyes still fixed on the train wreck before us.

Jordan snorts humorlessly, moving him gently back into his arms, and Navin snuggles closer. "We can't do anything, Nav. And even if we could, who would listen?"

And Jordan's right. Because this isn't the caricature kind of black-face that you'd see in an old minstrel show, so nobody we could complain to will feel like anything needs to be done. To them, Heather is simply a well-skilled makeup artist expressing her art. She's probably already filmed a tutorial for her channel.

And it doesn't help that her family has enough influence to just make it all go away.

The angry heat surging in my veins ratchets up in intensity.

We watch in silence as everyone in their little crowd by the large windows cheer and compliment Heather, the rugby guys practically chanting as she swings the bat back and forth like Beyoncé did in the music video.

145

"And what the hell is Marcus doing just standing there?" Quincy spits out.

I don't bother to contain my scoff, but it is disappointing to see Marcus doing that weird grimace-like smile of discomfort that some Black guys do when their white girlfriend does some racist nonsense. Because they think having a white girlfriend is too important to say anything.

"Okay, I'm going to end this," Quincy says, hefting out of the chair. "You coming, Jordie?"

Jordan nods, standing up and grabbing his crutches.

As they walk away, I turn to Kitan, whose eyes are fixed firmly out the window.

FIFTEEN

Kitan

In any given piece of music, there are transitions. They usually happen several times in one piece, meant to signal you to move from one section to the next. The task of the musician is to find the best way to make the transition smooth enough to keep the music flowing. Sometimes they slow down the last few notes at the end of the section, and then move on to the next.

So it's really strange how now, here in the Sixth Form common room, the world starts to slow down in front of my eyes. Because there's nothing particularly transitionary about this moment. It isn't different from what has been before. Heather is once again at the center of something, being praised and applauded; this is business as usual.

And yet, everything slows. Like wading underwater in a dream with every sound muffled. Because it's the first time I'm seeing Heather today and the sight is arresting.

Heather in blackface. Standing there performing for everyone what *she* thinks it all means.

I glance down at my thumb brushing slowly along the hem of my yellow cropped hoodie, the lines of folded brown skin shadowy in the grooves. I look up at her dress, mustard ruffles against the counterfeit shade.

The sudden press of Sarah's fingers on my palm, squeezing my hand in hers—safe—brings the world back into full speed.

I squeeze back.

But I can't look at Sarah, at anything, as my heart pounds hard in my chest. So I shift my gaze out the window at the gray stone bricks of Maudhill House far in the distance.

"Right, lads! I see you've all finished your lunch?" Quincy says suddenly from behind, but he doesn't wait for a response. "Brilliant. Let's get to the field, start prepping for the match."

There's a chorus of groans but they all start filing out of the common room. I glance over to see the uncomfortable expression on Marcus's face just before Quincy drags him out by the collar.

Good.

For a moment, Heather looks a little put out at the loss of her fans, but then she shrugs and heads over to join us.

She says something, something I can't hear, because Iyanu's words from Sunday dinner have taken over instead.

We don't want things to get worse.

I glance back out the window.

SIXTEEN

Iyanu

"Can everyone hear me?"

Jordan's voice comes in muffled through my wireless earbud, the sound distorted by the rowdy noises of the players, the high-pitched laughter from the kids, and the cheering crowd.

Adjusting the earbud, I look across the field to his distant form sitting on the bench.

"Yeah, we can hear you. You're just a little fuzzy though," Navin responds. He's much farther away, a tiny dot standing at the top of the steps of the sports center building, which sits at the end of the long path behind the spectators, waiting for the signal to go into the boys' changing room.

Jordan's voice comes through again, clearer this time. "Better?"

"Yup," I say, lifting the viewfinder to my eye and zooming in to where he's sitting.

He looks up from his phone just as Quincy approaches him.

"Is everyone on? You called the group chat, right?" Quincy's voice is a lot more distant, but the mic picks it up, and Jordan nods in response. "Awesome. Okay, I'm going to head back onto the field now, gonna try and keep Luc up on the far end for as long as possible."

Quincy leans closer to Jordan, collecting the other earbud from its case and putting it into his own ear. "Navin?" he asks, voice clearer now.

"Yeah?"

"You've got this. I would make a speech about how this is your mission and you've chosen to accept it, but I feel like that would be a bit much."

Jordan laughs. "Just saying that is already too much, bro."

Quincy smacks him upside the head, and I can't help the giggle that escapes me.

"You okay there, Iyanu?"

I freeze at Mrs. Tarar's words, lowering my camera and slowly turning around with as innocent a smile as I can muster.

"All good, Miss!"

She smirks, clearly unconvinced, but decides to let it drop. "I'm going to head to the other side of the field and get some more shots . . ."

But the guys are still talking, and I can't concentrate on what she's saying.

Stretching out a nonexistent kink in my neck, I subtly remove the earbud.

". . . I want to see how you deal with the light coming through there, okay?"

I glance over to the far side of the field where she's pointing at the willows along the lakeside, excitement thrumming at the way the sun casts their shadows across the grass.

"Sure!"

Then Mrs. Tarar crosses the field and I quickly put the earbud back in.

"Sorry, guys, that was Mrs. Tarar."

"It's okay, we heard," Quincy says. "I was just telling Navin that you've got his six."

My grin widens. "How many spy films did you watch to prepare for this? Breathe if it's more than five."

His silence is answer enough.

"Okay," Jordan says, bringing us back into focus. "We've got about twenty minutes before halftime. It's not a real match so we're all just gonna stay out here and hang with the kids. But hopefully Nav will be out by then."

"Don't worry, I got this," Navin responds.

"All right, I'm off," Quincy says. "Do your thing."

Then he takes out the earbud and runs back onto the field, picking up a giggling Hanwood kid with pigtails as she receives the ball before running her to the other side.

I pointedly ignore the warmth building in my stomach.

"Okay, I'm going in," Navin declares.

I zoom in on the sports center doors just as he disappears through them, feeling a thrill at the plan underway.

"Okay." Navin's voice echoes a little now that he's inside. "Which one's The Locker again, Jordan?"

Jordan starts to explain, but there's a sudden motion in my periphery. Turning to the other side of the field I find Mrs. Tarar waving at me. She gestures to the trees and then back at the field again.

"Oh yeah," I whisper.

Half listening to the conversation as Jordan directs Navin to Luc's locker, I head over to the willows. Once I lift the camera back to my eye, it instantly becomes clear that Mrs. Tarar was right. The light from here is perfect.

"Iyanu? Where'd you go?"

I turn the lens from the players back to Jordan on the bench who's now looking all around him.

"Over by the willows. Miss wants me to take photos from here. I'll be back to my post in a second."

He sighs. "Oh yeah, okay, I'll keep an eye out. Quincy's got Luc covered for now anyway."

I nod though he can't see me. "Navin? How're things looking?"

Navin huffs, a sound of rustling fabric joining his frustration. "I can't find my lock pick . . ."

"Why do you even have a lock pick anyway?" Jordan asks incredulously.

"Don't ask questions you don't want the answers to."

A relic from old Navin it seems.

". . . yes!" The sound of metal scraping on metal, and then Navin's soft humming as he picks the lock.

Chuckling softly, I turn the lens back to the players.

It's funny watching all these big, burly players running around the field with tiny little humans weaving between them. They seem to have abandoned most of the proper rules. Whenever things go wrong (read: whenever someone wants to cheat), the guys pick up whichever kid has the ball to run them across the field. Or when someone tries to take the ball from a Hanwood kid, three to four of them act as a human shield.

I watch them run around for a few minutes, waiting for the right moment to capture. Quincy is never too far from Luc, who's too focused on the game to notice and shouting orders or plays or whatever to keep the game going. He makes a good captain, but you can tell that he's still finding his feet; each time he shouts an order, it's like he's unsure if they'll follow. Maybe he knows the guys still see Jordan as their leader.

Adjusting the zoom, I turn the lens to the crowd only for Heather's face to fill the shot.

The anger surges again, so I shift back to Quincy, and it's just as well, because the sun seems to have had the same idea.

Perfect.

He catches the ball midair and I click the shutter.

When his feet touch the ground again, he instantly looks around, finding one of the kids and tossing the ball to her. She grins wide, breaking into a run with Quincy shielding her all the way up the field.

The other players cheer, even the ones on the opposite team, and I know that look in their eyes. Jordan might be their captain and Marcus might be the star, but much like he is with the twins, Quincy is their anchor. He has their respect and their trust.

Turning my back to the field I clutch tightly at my camera strap, breathing through the emotion, the memories.

Get it together.

Lady Chalford stands in the distance on the far side of the lake, and on the other edge lies the large stone structure of Aestas Bower—one of the four round domed pavilions situated throughout the seven hundred acres of gardens surrounding Wodebury Hall.

I lift the camera to my eye, making sure the pavilion is framed perfectly in the shot.

The piercing sound of Mr. Forrester's whistle jolts me out of my focus, and it's only then that I realize Navin's gentle humming has stopped.

I look around the field desperately. It's halftime and Navin is nowhere to be found. "Where's Nav?"

There's a loud rustle before Jordan's voice comes through my earbud.

"No idea. Mr. Roberts walked into the changing room a few minutes ago. He took his earphones out, muted his end, and hasn't said anything since."

The beginnings of panic start to creep in.

I glance around the field again to find Quincy on the far side with three Hanwood kids, trying to wrangle them over to get refreshments. He waves frantically at me, then lifts his hands up in confusion, clearly asking where Navin is.

"Come over here, Q!" Jordan shouts.

But one of the boys tugs at Quincy's shirt and he has to attend to him.

My panic climbs a little higher.

Just then, a loud crackling comes in through my earbud before a breathless Navin starts speaking.

"Oh gosh. Mr. Roberts just left. Guess this whole fake-dating thing wasn't such a bad idea because I was able to cover by saying I was grabbing something for Jordan."

Relief floods through me and I chuckle at the self-satisfaction in Navin's voice.

"Have you found anything?" Jordan asks, a strange shift in his tone.

But I can't probe at it further because a quick movement flashes in my periphery. It's Luc's reflective captain armband glinting in the sunlight as he weaves through the team toward—

"Jordan! Luc's heading to the sports center!"

But just as Jordan registers what I've said, Luc walks right past him, heading to the path behind the spectators.

Navin squeaks. "What? No! Someone stall him. I can't do—"

His side of the call cuts off.

The pounding in my chest increases.

Jordan is struggling to rise to his feet, looking around for his crutches and calling out to Luc. But Luc doesn't listen, of course, considering everything that's happened.

Panicked, I look to Quincy who's just noticed what's going on. But he's even farther away from Luc, and the kids are demanding his attention.

My feet move of their own accord, and I practically fly across the field toward the path to the building.

"Luc!"

I catch up to him halfway up the path and he turns to me with a frown.

"What do you want?"

Luckily, my mouth seems to have it covered where my brain is losing the plot. "I-I'm taking a quick group shot for the newsletter. Don't you want to be in it?"

His frown deepens. "Can't you just do it after the game?"

"It's just . . . the lighting!" I say, remembering the sun through the willows. Hopefully, an appeal to his vanity will work. "It's perfect right now, and who knows what it's gonna be like once the game is over. You know how it is, you do photography."

Luc seems to think it over for a moment then sighs. "Fine."

"Oh, thank God," Jordan whispers, then ends the call.

After heading back to the field, I get everyone into the perfect positions for the shot, but I'm barely paying attention, still too on edge for Navin.

"Okay, everyone smile," I say, lifting the viewfinder to my eye.

They all do, and I try to breathe past my worry. Luckily, the sun seems to be on my side today, because the lighting *is* perfect, enhancing the warm tones of the few brown-skinned faces dotted throughout the group.

Satisfied with the balance, I take the photo.

"All right, folks, second half!" Mr. Forrester calls out, his white face red-cheeked as he blows the whistle again before turning to me. "Great stuff, Iyanu. I look forward to seeing all the photos when you're done."

"Thanks, Sir."

As soon as Mr. Forrester jogs away, I hurry back up the path to the sports center, getting to the bottom of the stairs just as Navin slips out the doors at the top. A few seconds later, Jordan comes up from behind me.

"What happened? Did you find anything?" I ask hurriedly between breaths, dread already filling my chest at the sight of his empty hands. "My negatives?"

Joining us on ground level, Navin sighs.

"I couldn't search through all of it because of Mr. Roberts," he says, nose wrinkling. "But I managed to write down some of the stuff in my notes app that I saw. There were loads of dated envelopes and folders with things in them. I was in a rush of course, but I sort of jumped around between them so we could have a good spread of info from the different envelopes. I figured some of it could at least help us flesh out the murder board?" Then he meets my gaze with disappointed eyes. "But your negative binder wasn't there."

SEVENTEEN

Kitan

"How come neither of you liked my outfit post?"

Sarah and I share a quick glance as Heather tucks her phone into her purse before looking at us.

The field is slowly emptying of spectators now that the kids have left, and the boys' rugby team is making their way to the changing rooms. I really just want to talk to Marcus, not deal with Heather's . . . Heathering.

We don't want things to get worse.

Tugging on the frayed ends of my shorts, I try to pull together the right thing to say.

But maybe Heather wasn't expecting an answer to her question because she just carries on. "Will you at least share the makeup tutorial when I put it up on my channel tonight?"

For some reason, I think about Gabriel Towne and Heather's upcoming collaboration with them. Would they see it?

I throw Sarah another look, and she sends one of support back.

"I . . . didn't see the post," I say, swallowing down the discomfort in my throat. "I was pretty busy in the music department so I couldn't check my phone. Did you get a lot of likes?"

Heather snorts.

"Yeah, like always." She pauses, eyeing my outfit appreciatively. "We haven't seen each other at all today. You look amazing."

It comes automatically. The happiness I feel at her praise. But it's tempered instantly by the heavy feeling inside.

"But of course you do, *you've* got the body for it. Genetic advantage, I guess. Oh! Let's take a photo together. Two Beyoncés. The post will probably blow up even more. Gabriel Towne will love it."

I blink.

I'm not sure what to say to that. And compartmentalizing doesn't seem to work this time.

"Did you get a lot of comments?"

Heather nods, frowning slightly. "Yeah. Most of them were great, but there were some annoying trolls saying that I shouldn't have done it. Like, hello? I don't have to be Black to dress up like Beyoncé. Quincy literally dressed up like a rat. It doesn't matter, it's just a costume."

A costume.

I let out a tiny breath, pleased that at least she brought it up first, but I can practically hear Iyanu's voice in my head screaming *It's not the same! At all!*

"I think, maybe, those people were talking about your makeup? It's a little too . . . dark?"

Heather's frown deepens, and she tucks a curl behind her ear as the winter breeze blows it into her face. Before she can respond though, Sarah speaks.

"I saw the comments. Kitan's right."

"So you did see the post?" Heather retorts.

And Iyanu screams again, *That's what you got from all that?*

Heather continues. "But I look great with a tan."

Sarah sighs. "Yeah, you do. But this isn't a tan," she says, gesturing to Heather's face.

As they go back and forth, I wrap my arms around my middle and let myself retreat.

I just want to talk to Marcus. I don't want to be here.

Everything feels too unsteady.

"Maybe it would be better if you just didn't put up the tutorial."

At Sarah's suggestion, I turn back to them, clenching my sides to stop my hands shaking.

Heather lets out a tired breath then grips my arm gently, holding my gaze. I try not to flinch. "Will that make you feel better? Because I'd never want you to be uncomfortable."

Never want me to be uncomfortable.

I stare at her for a moment, wondering about the "trolls" in the comments, the people who felt like they couldn't comment, and the ones who loved the post.

It's not just about me, or the tutorial video. Not posting it won't solve the actual problem.

Was that Iyanu's voice or mine?

"It would be a good idea not to post it."

Heather looks annoyed, clearly not wanting to discuss this anymore.

"Fine." Then she pulls out her phone, quickly typing something. "Anyway, I need to get changed and ready for the head girl workshop. I'll see you both later."

Sarah's expression twists, but it barely lasts a moment before she nods.

"Same. I just need to quickly sort something out with Oliver." She spares me a short apologetic glance before turning back to Heather. "But hey, my new pearl necklace arrived yesterday. Maybe we can both wear ours for the workshop?"

An olive branch.

Heather looks at Sarah for a second, assessing, then smiles. "Sure, sounds good."

As they head off in opposite directions, Heather toward the lake to Lady Chalford and Sarah in the direction of the Wodebury House courtyard, I can't help but hope that we never have to have this conversation with Heather again.

Ever since the new swimming pool was added to the sports center building, it always smells like chlorine, so as I draw closer to the boys' changing room, the scent combines with the fog of body spray into a noxious gas.

The building itself is a combination of old and new. Stone Victorian foundations with inner workings of glass and industrial steel that houses the best equipment and technologies sports science offers. Its refurbishment was the first in the long line of projects that Heather's father's patronage would provide the Wodebury sports department.

I round the corner to the boys' changing room just as the last horde of them bustle out into the hallway. Panicking, I move closer to the wall.

I *had* waited for Marcus to come out so we could speak in private without anyone seeing me, but then I'd remembered that Marcus is always the last one to leave. Always takes the extra time to make sure he looks perfect, and I couldn't wait any longer. I need to find out about this bet to get my head right for the performance tomorrow evening.

As the group of players walk past, I keep my head down, but none of them pay me any mind.

I feel a strange pang.

It's good that they didn't notice me because I really want to be discreet about this. But it's yet another example of the ways that the Polaroids have changed everything. Before they were released, those players would have called out to me in greeting.

I push open the changing room door.

Unfortunately, the noxious gas is thicker in here, but as expected, it's empty save for Marcus, who's standing by his locker scrolling through his phone. He's already half-dressed, a white undershirt tucked into checkered navy suit trousers.

"Marcus."

Letting out a yelp, he jumps a foot into the air, swiveling around with his phone brandished like a sword.

"Kitan!" he says, clutching at his chest. "What the hell?"

I eye the device for a moment, and he flushes, putting the phone down on the bench in front of him. His hands shake a little as he grabs the button-up hanging in his locker, and I feel a tiny burst of guilt. With his anxiety, Marcus is always on edge anyway.

"Sorry, I didn't mean to scare you. You told me we could talk after the game."

"It's fine," he says gruffly, slipping into the pristine blue shirt. "I just thought we'd meet in Brookfield or something. You know this is the boys' changing room, right?"

I shrug. "Well, it's only you in here."

Besides, this way you can't dodge me.

"Fair enough," Marcus says, chuckling with an eye roll, then grabs his gold-striped Premiership tie from the hanger. "What's up? Sorry, I've been a bit busy these last couple days."

I lean against the bench railing, watching as he twists the silk tie into a knot.

"The Polaroids have ruined a lot of things," I start. "Sarah's pretty upset that you two aren't going to the ball together anymore."

At that Marcus snorts, a tired mirthless sound.

"Maybe she shouldn't have cheated on me then."

From the way he avoids my eyes as he whispers the words, it's clear that he doesn't fully believe them.

"Sarah wouldn't cheat on anyone. I *know* you know that." I continue, "Whoever did this just wanted to mess everything up, so they lied about a bunch of people."

If only that was the case with mine.

Marcus shrugs again, but I can see the vulnerability behind his eyes.

"Whatever, it doesn't matter," he mumbles. "It's not like we were in love. It was just a fun matchmaking thing."

"But you'd been talking—you said you liked her, and now you're just going with Heather?" I ask, completely dumbfounded. This isn't him. "And what about what she did today? Why are you still going to go with her?"

At this, his eyes flash to mine. "The same reason that you're still friends with her."

There's a long silence as we both stare at each other, and something passes through the air between us that makes my skin prickle with discomfort.

I break the stare first, eyes falling to the gold stripes of his tie. "I need you to tell me everything you know about the bet."

I meet his eyes again just as Marcus's expression switches to wary surprise, then quickly settles on neutral curiosity.

"What bet?"

I raise a brow. "Seriously?"

He shifts on his feet, hands fidgeting for a moment before he hurriedly grabs a small bristle brush from his gym bag and then heads toward the shower area. I follow after him, rounding the corner carefully so my boots don't slip on the wet tiles.

"Come on, Marcus."

He stands in front of the sinks, focusing resolutely on his reflection in the mirror as he brushes the sides of his undercut.

"I don't know anything about it."

But we both know he's lying.

"Who did Oliver make the bet with?"

Continuing to avoid my gaze, Marcus huffs, turning on the tap to wash his hands.

After a few minutes of silence I join him by the sinks, placing a hand on his where it now rests against the counter. His fingers are still wet, but they're warm, and I squeeze tight.

"Please, Marcus."

It takes a few moments as he stares at our joined hands, before finally turning his gaze to mine, and the resolve leaks from his light brown eyes.

"Luc."

I blink once. Twice.

"What?"

My heart races, fueled by the confusion in my mind.

"Oliver made the bet with Luc."

"Why?" I ask in disbelief. "I don't understand. What would he get out of it? And why didn't you tell me?"

Marcus squeezes my hand, but I snatch it away.

"Because it was just stupid. I didn't even remember that it happened," he says. "It was after a game a couple weeks ago. We went to the Roweton common room for the after-party. And you know how we get. I don't remember how, but Luc and Oliver got into it. It was just a stupid bet. It didn't matter."

And those words spark my confusion to anger, heating my face like tinder. It's like everything I was too shaken to express when Heather walked into the common room comes spilling out now.

I swivel around to face him.

"It doesn't matter?" I ground out. "Making me look stupid doesn't matter?"

But Marcus takes a tiny step back, and the fire instantly evaporates.

I don't react like this. I never lose my temper.

Especially not with Marcus. No matter how betrayed I feel.

Why does everything have to *feel* so much now? Why can't I just sift through the bad stuff anymore?

The harsh burn of tears fills my throat, and I breathe through the ache.

"Treating me like a joke . . . It doesn't matter?"

Marcus steps forward sheepishly. "I didn't mean it like that. I just thought you liked Oliver. At the matchmaking event it came down to you and some other girl, right? And he chose you because he made the bet."

Exactly.

A mirthless laugh escapes my lips.

He would never understand.

Still, I say, "And what's the point if it's not real?"

Marcus's face scrunches in confusion, and he opens his mouth to speak, but I'm sick of this. I don't want to talk about this with someone who clearly doesn't understand.

"So what you're saying is that a whole bunch of the guys knew about the bet? Anyone could have released the Polaroids?"

He runs a hand down his face. "I guess so. But, Kitan, honestly, nobody really cared. Oliver and Luc haven't gotten along ever since they had to room together in Year Seven. So most of us just ignored them. It was an after-party—we were just chilling."

I search Marcus's eyes, checking for any signs of deceit, but he seems to be telling the truth.

"Which one is Luc's locker?"

"His locker?"

My frustration flares again, but I tamp it back down.

"No, we're not doing that again. I know about The Locker. It's Luc's secret stash place and some of the other rugby guys use it too. It's not as secret as they all think it is," I say, allowing myself to feel a little smug. "I need answers, so I'm going to need something to get Luc to talk to me."

Marcus does that fidgeting thing again, and I sigh.

"No one will know you told me where it is. I don't want anyone to know what I'm doing anyway. It'll be our little secret."

A short pause.

"Fine."

Marcus leads me back to his locker.

"I said *The* Locker. Not yours."

He throws me a withering look. "I *know*. I just have to get something. How were you planning on opening it? Sheer force of will?"

He chuckles when I smack his arm, then slides open a loose panel at the back of the locker and pulls out a key.

"Luc doesn't know I have a copy."

"I promise, I won't tell. But how come you have it?"

Marcus sighs. "I can't do anything to make them stop, I've tried. But I know how this works, and I'm not going to let them switch things up on me so the Black kids take the fall if there's ever trouble. No matter how close Luc was to Jordan and me, the others are another story. I figured the least I could do was make sure they can't hurt me or my brothers."

I sigh this time. "All right."

The Locker is seven doors down from Marcus's in the farthest corner of the room from the door. Quickly slotting in the key and opening it, he takes a step back and gestures me forward.

"Have at it. But please be quick."

It's neater than I'd expected, complete with IKEA workspace dividers and everything.

The top section holds various things: stacks of cards, a tin box with an inkpad and rubber stamps in it, several old pay-as-you-go phones, and brown A4 envelopes with letters and numbers that look like dates written on them.

I inspect the envelopes first. The letters and numbers have disconnected square corners around them in faded ink, so it's likely they were done using the inkpad and stamps to obscure handwriting.

A cursory peek into a few of the envelopes tell me that they mostly contain jewelry, USB sticks, small items of clothing, and other knickknacks that I can't even begin to assign ownership to, so I reluctantly move to the middle section. This houses several magazine files stuffed to the brim with more envelopes also labeled with letters and dates.

I turn to Marcus, needing a way to narrow down the search. "What's in the envelopes?"

"I dunno. Screenshots, pictures, notes, stuff like that." He glances over his shoulder at the door. "You've got to be quick about this. Everyone's gone to the food tech labs because Quincy made desserts. They'll get suspicious if I don't show up eventually."

Huffing, I kneel down to look through the bottom level. This section seems to serve its intended function—Luc's rugby boots and gym bag its only occupants.

"Come on, Kitan," Marcus says from above.

"Fine, fine."

Grabbing the bag, I pull it open, holding my breath against the awful smell that wafts out.

Eww.

As expected, inside is just a filthy rugby kit, so I quickly zip it back up and return to the first level while Marcus starts tapping nervously on the side of the locker.

I look through the brown envelopes, starting with the date closest to today and work my way backward.

Come on . . .

When I get to the envelope with the date of the matchmaking event on it, I grab it, pouring out its contents.

What?

A long string of shiny pearls.

EIGHTEEN

Iyanu

Finding the negatives in Luc's locker was a long shot, but not finding them still hurts, and I just want to be alone. So when everyone heads to the food tech lab for the desserts that Quincy made, I head to the photography lab to develop the film from the game. It's likely to be free, considering all the Career Day stuff and it's a half day.

And I should probably start looking through my old negative binders to find other photos for the article.

Even as I think it, I know I won't. The photos in those binders are random shots from around the school. Nowhere near good enough to write an article that'll land me this job. Not the way the ones from the fair will.

But my hopes for solitude disintegrate when I turn the corner.

Oliver and Sarah are arguing in Mandarin on the far side of the classroom, beams of sunlight pouring in from the windows beside them.

I pause in the doorway, unsure of what to do. Their words go right over my head, but it still feels like I'm intruding.

". . . Luc, Heather . . . Kitan . . ."

Registering the familiar names, my brain automatically tries to pull some more from Sarah's angry words, but Oliver scoffs, and it halts her speech. Hoisting his satchel over his shoulder, he spits out some final words before turning.

Their eyes flash with surprise as they find me standing there, and a long silence follows.

"Sorry, I just got here," I finish weakly.

"No worries," Oliver says, looking sheepish, then rushes past me out the door.

Another awkward silence, but this time Sarah turns her back to me, pulling off the barrister wig, and I hear her soft sniffling and gasping breaths.

"Umm." I step a little farther into the room. "Are you okay?"

I wince at the ridiculous question. She's obviously not.

Sarah chuckles wetly. "Yeah, it's all right."

She turns around, mascara slightly smudged around her eyes, and I slowly move to join her.

"Sorry. I didn't think anyone would be in here."

Sarah shrugs, an uncomfortable stuttered motion.

"You came to use the darkroom?"

"The film closet and the developer room, actually."

She glances at the two doorways on the other side of the classroom. One leads to an airy room with a deep sink where we develop our film into negatives, the other is a pitch-black closet where we unload our cameras to begin the process. "Okay, I'll let you get on with it then."

But she makes no move to leave, and from the way her eyes are darting around the room, she has something to say, but is too nervous to speak.

Her and Oliver were arguing about the group. They were talking about Luc. If she knows something, maybe today doesn't have to be a total waste.

"Is everything really okay?" I ask softly.

Her eyes finally meet mine. "I'm sorry about Heather. Her . . ."

She gestures generally at her face.

Oh.

A surprised smile tugs at my lips.

"Thanks. I mean, *you* don't have to apologize. But it's nice that . . . yeah."

Another brief silence.

I have to play this right.

"Is Oliver okay?" I ask, gesturing over my shoulder. "I don't think I've ever seen him that upset."

Her expression crumples in frustration, and for a second, I think I've blown it. But then she sighs.

"Just all the stuff with Kitan. God, everything is such a mess."

She scrubs a hand down her face with a groan, resting her elbows on the desk. When she looks up again, her eyes glaze over to the middle distance.

"Seeing Heather and Marcus together . . ." She trails off, rubbing at her arm. "I could tell she was jealous when we started talking. But I liked him, I just couldn't bring myself to care about how she felt."

She pauses, shaking her head.

"But of course, in the end, he ditches me for her."

I know you cheated on Marcus.

That was her Polaroid message.

But before my thoughts can run away from me, Sarah's eyes refocus and she meets mine, expression somehow both exhausted and bitter. "I guess Heather always gets what she wants."

The realization clicks into place. "You think Heather released the Polaroids."

Sarah glances away. "All I know is that when Heather got here in Year Nine, she took over everything. She dated Luc, who was the best player back then, and it instantly made her popular. But then out of nowhere, Marcus suddenly eclipsed Luc. So she dropped Luc and shifted her sights to Marcus." Sarah shrugs, but there's nothing nonchalant about the tense set of her shoulders. "I guess she's just been waiting for the right moment ever since. I'd hoped she'd let it go when she saw I had actual feelings for Marcus. But now because of the Polaroids, she's finally got him."

I hurriedly analyze what she's saying.

On the one hand, Heather broke it off with Quincy because of the Polaroids. They ruined something for her, so she's been farther down the list of suspects. But if Sarah's right, then Heather never cared about being with Quincy, and the Polaroids landed her the perfect opportunity to get what she's been after this whole time.

In this new context, Heather is actually the only one who's come out of all of this happy. Everyone else's life is a mess.

Especially mine. Because everyone's blaming me for this.

Sarah holds my gaze again, seemingly realizing all the things she's said, and her expression creases with worry.

"Don't worry, I won't tell Heather."

Her relieved sigh breaks my heart a little more, and it worsens when her expression completely transforms into a happy smile as she waves. "I'll see you later, Iyanu."

How long can Sarah pretend? How long can she stay friends with Heather?

How long can Kitan?

"See you later."

And with that, she leaves.

I make quick work of unloading my film in the closet, head swimming with the new information. When I step out, Quincy is walking into the classroom.

"Knock, knock."

His grin fades once he sees the look on my face, and he rushes in, carefully balancing a dish in his hands.

"What is it? What happened?"

I take a beat too long to respond and Quincy's eyes fill with worry.

"Is it because the negatives weren't there?" he asks, placing the dish on the table. "Because we can try and break into the locker again. Or Luc's room. It's not over yet, we've still got time."

Ten days till the deadline.

The reminder stings.

Then a sudden, terrifying thought jumps to the front of my mind.

If Heather did this . . .

"What if they got rid of the negatives? Threw them away?"

Heather would destroy them.

Quincy steps closer. "Let's not go there yet. We don't know that."

But we don't *not* know that.

My heart is racing now, pulsing between my ears, and I grip my camera strap tightly.

A small part of my mind recognizes that I'm catastrophizing, but I hadn't even stopped to consider it before. Either Luc did this and he *might* have thrown them away. Or Heather did this, and they've *definitely* been thrown away. Either way, the Black Girls Winter Fair negatives could be *gone* gone.

"Think about it, Yaya. They took the photos you'd printed from the matchmaking event with them, but they didn't stop there. They took all your negatives as well. So there has to be a reason other than just throwing them away."

I nod shakily. "Sarah was just here. She thinks it could've been Heather. Heather could actually be a suspect. She hates me, Q!"

Suddenly Quincy is right there, stepping in close to me and taking my cheeks into his warm palms.

My lungs squeeze tight.

His eyes are so wide and brown, filled with such a determined certainty that I can't look away even if I wanted to.

"It's okay. Breathe. Breathe." His thumbs dance lightly over my cheekbones, my jawline, the tips of my ears, and back again, leaving fire in their wake. "This was just the first try. We still have time to try something else."

I take in a deep breath.

But as the much-needed air finally flows down into my lungs, I catch the heady scent of chocolate from Quincy's sleeves. And it's not just any chocolate, it's his special melted chocolate that's mixed with some ingredient he'd dubbed "The Secret Sauce." A scent that I haven't smelled in so long.

"You made He Loves, She Loves cookies?"

Quincy's expression goes from gentle concern to bewildered amusement, head falling back with the force of his laughter.

"I can't with you. You were just—" He shakes his head to himself as he chuckles. "Yes. I also brought some milk. Lactose-free, of course," he says, pulling out a silver flask from his back pocket. "Shall we?"

I clear my throat. "Sure."

He sets down the flask and rests his hands on my shoulders again.

"It'll be okay, Yaya. Just forget about Heather and let's focus on our main target. We can figure all this out." Then he steers me to the table, and I settle down on one of the stools, placing my things on the one next to me.

I watch as Quincy sets up the cookies, large hands delicate as he pours some steaming milk into the lid of the flask, before folding two napkins on the table with a sharp point like we're at some grand dinner.

"Voilà!"

Chuckling, I grab one of the warm cookies.

Maybe if I'd been less all over the place because of the Luc/Heather debacle, I would have been more prepared. But I'm not. And so my first bite of He Loves, She Loves cookies after three years almost has me tearing up. I don't even bother to hold in a groan, eyes squeezing closed as I lean down over the table, an aching nostalgia filling me.

Quincy chuckles. "Glad to see you still love them."

I look up, unable to contain my smile. "'She Loves,' remember?"

"Very true."

The dessert is Quincy's own creation. Vanilla cookies filled with melted dark chocolate. One half dipped in a milk chocolate glaze, the other in caramel, and sweet honeycomb crumbled on top. He'd created them on the Sunday afternoon of one of our movie marathons. That weekend, the theme was Old Hollywood, and it was the first time we watched *Funny Face*. At the end of the film, Fred Astaire sang a song called "He Loves and She Loves." Being the nerd that he is, Quincy was inspired and came to school the following day with cookies that were a combination of our favorite flavors. Half milk chocolate and honeycomb for me, half dark chocolate and caramel for him. It's exactly the kind of questionable treat a thirteen-year-old would create to satisfy their sweet tooth, but I can't get enough of them. And from then on, anything Old Hollywood reminded me of Quincy and these cookies.

"Thanks for bringing these," I say, hoping he can both sense and not sense everything I'm feeling.

"No problem."

We eat in silence, dunking the desserts in the warm milk until all six cookies are gone.

"Okay," I say, rising to my feet, "I need to get started on these photos."

"Wait, one sec. You've got . . ."

Quincy grabs a clean napkin, wetting it in the sink in the developer room before taking my hands in his.

I stand frozen, heart pounding as he carefully wipes the chocolate from my hands. It's easy, the way our fingers weave together as he cleans between mine, the same rich brown skin streaked with sunlight from the window next to us.

And then it's over.

"There you go." He huffs out a laugh. "Maybe I should put less melted chocolate in those."

Slightly breathless, I drop my hands out of sight at my sides, flexing my fingers to stop the tingling. "Never."

And that makes him laugh again.

After grabbing my things, I head back over to develop the film and Quincy follows close behind. He then sits down on a stool in the corner to watch the process. I try not to feel too self-conscious at the heavy gaze following each step, but eventually a comfortable silence settles around us.

"I should come back when you print the photos. It'll be like that *Funny Face* scene when Fred and Audrey are in the darkroom, and he's printing her pictures."

I smile, nodding. "Well, in that analogy, you're Audrey Hepburn's character, and considering you also have a funny face, I suppose it works."

Quincy clutches at his chest with a faux wounded expression.

"Hey! It's not my fault that my eyebrows have a mind of their own," he says, then smirks. "Besides, funny face or not, as I recall, you loved taking photos of it."

The wide smile on his face tells me it's a joke, but my brain sends a jolting message to my mouth to change the subject, stalling the heartache of those memories.

"It's hilarious because 'I have a funny face' was Audrey's character's thing. But Fred Astaire actually had a pretty funny face."

Quincy chuckles. "A *Black*face in that other film he did."

He says the words just as I'm about to clip the negative strip to the drying line, and my hands slip, but I quickly catch it.

"Eww, don't remind me. It was so wrong. I don't think I've ever switched off a film so quickly." When I finally peg the negative up on the line and look back at Quincy's face, his expression is sober and I just know he's about to bring up Heather.

"Hey, don't say that. We all need representation."

The sound of the snort that escapes my lips as I double over with laughter would be embarrassing, but I'm too focused on trying to breathe as my lungs gasp for air. Quincy's cackles join mine.

"Oh my God. Why are you like this?"

I wipe the moisture from my eyes, and he follows suit before speaking. "But seriously, I can't believe Heather."

I roll my eyes. "And don't get me started on Marcus just standing there basically cosigning it."

"Don't worry, I'm planning to rip into him."

My frustration builds as I think about it.

"Kitan was sitting right there looking *amazing* as Beyoncé, but it's like she was invisible."

We both kiss our teeth at the same time, and I meet his eyes, unable to help my chuckle as he does the same.

"Heather just looked so ridiculous. Swinging the bat around like she was signaling a plane."

Another loud snort of giggles escapes my lips. "A hot mess."

Quincy sighs.

"Why did we even choose that theme for the marathon that weekend anyway?" I ask, starting to clean up the equipment. "Like, how did we even have the attention span for those ridiculously long Old Hollywood scenes?"

Quincy chuckles again. "I don't know about you, but I just remember not wanting you to go home. You going home meant that the weekend was over. I'd have watched anything."

After all the day's activities, Dad asking for a calm painting session when I get home is just what I need. So it isn't until a few minutes after Mum walks into the studio that I realize I'm being ambushed.

Shoveling spoonfuls of fudge brownie ice cream into her mouth, Mum comes over to stand between our easels, taking a closer look at our canvases.

Dad's request had seemed innocent enough. Help him draw the sketch for the oil painting he was going to do next ("A father-daughter piece, Iyanu. It'll be great!") while he finishes up another piece. He works as a curator in the modern art gallery in town, but he's also an artist in his own right, and so we often work together. Nothing out of the ordinary.

Dad puts down his brush and I glance over. He's only halfway